THE "OH NO" TRIO

A SEALO OF ASTARA ADVENTURE

By

J.L. ALONZO

iUniverse, Inc.
New York Bloomington

The "Oh No" Trio
A Sealo of Astara Adventure

Copyright © 2010 J.L. Alonzo

All rights reserved. No part of this book may be used or reproduced by any means, graphic, electronic, or mechanical, including photocopying, recording, taping or by any information storage retrieval system without the written permission of the publisher except in the case of brief quotations embodied in critical articles and reviews.

This is a work of fiction. All of the characters, names, incidents, organizations, and dialogue in this novel are either the products of the author's imagination or are used fictitiously.

iUniverse books may be ordered through booksellers or by contacting:

iUniverse
1663 Liberty Drive
Bloomington, IN 47403
www.iuniverse.com
1-800-Authors (1-800-288-4677)

Because of the dynamic nature of the Internet, any Web addresses or links contained in this book may have changed since publication and may no longer be valid. The views expressed in this work are solely those of the author and do not necessarily reflect the views of the publisher, and the publisher hereby disclaims any responsibility for them.

ISBN: 978-1-4502-5460-1 (pbk)
ISBN: 978-1-4502-5461-8 (ebk)

Printed in the United States of America

iUniverse rev. date: 9/8/10

To all my students and friends
who read and critique my stories
and encourage me to continue writing.

Cast of Characters

Sealo — Thirteen year old nephew of Risan, the Lord of Astara.

Myra — Seven year old adopted child of Risan and Ela.

Shar — Fourteen year old ward of Risan, Lord of Astara.

Risan — Lord of Astara.

Ela — Mate of the Lord of Astara.

Shanar — Brother of the Lord of Astara.

Sosja — Mother of Sealo and sister of Risan.

Kanol — Father of Risan, Sosja, and Shanar. Grandfather of Sealo.

Ulena — Daughter of the Sage of Sho, a settlement devoted to the growing of herbs for Natural Healers.

Introduction

A long time ago on a star far away there was a kingdom where peace was always present. The beings of Astara were very enlightened and love was the basis of all life. All needs were met through mutual manifestation. There was no scarcity, hunger, homelessness, or violence. All beings lived in their hearts and cared for one another.

Children were cherished for their vitality and ingenuity. They were encouraged to explore their potential and exercise their imagination. They were cared for by all and loved for themselves with no preconceived expectations.

The Elders were honored for their wisdom and lived long productive lives of service. The beings of this world lived to be as much as two hundred years old. When the time came for separation from a lifetime, the beings ascended into the light to return later to live again, remembering all the lifetimes that came before.

Lord Risan of this kingdom was a wise and caring being whose heart was so big he could include any who came to the kingdom. With Ela, his mate, he oversaw the happenings of all. Harmony and happiness filled their world. Risan's household was a large Complex of people and buildings. Sosja, Risan's sister and her child, Sealo, lived at the Complex. Shar and Myra, two children from other worlds, had been adopted into Risan's family when they were very young and were the constant companions of Sealo.

This was a household of ambassadors, teachers, and healers, which extended from the Reber Sea to the rolling hills that bordered the Great Meadow. Risan's Complex nestled not far from the sea on a lush green plateau. The buildings of the Complex included the main housing and dining area, the Learning Center, the Healing Center, and the Temple. Their world was abundant with the natural things the universe offers. The buildings were arranged as to invite the beings to live in love.

The Council was the main decision making body for the kingdom. Risan and Shanar, his brother, were members. Risan also represented his kingdom in the greater Star System Council. Many travelers came to the kingdom. These visitors attended the Learning Center, worked or sought help at the Healing Center, worshipped at the Temple, and attended many meals and meetings in the Great Hall of the housing area.

It is in this room we will begin our story.

One

All we could see were feet as we crawled beneath the table in the Great Hall. The court meal had begun and many ambassadors from far away were gathered at Risan's grand tables. Many fascinating dishes were being served, for there were many beings from star systems with cultures very different from our own. We moved slowly, motioning to each other about the direction we would take next. Shar motioned left. Myra motioned right. I shook my head and motioned straight. We moved undeviating toward the head table and Ela's chair, which was located next to Risan's. We knew there would be consequences if Risan caught us but we continued. Then, for a split second, we froze. The feet next to us were shuffling and the guest was removing her red, high heel sandals. Ever ready to create excitement, Myra and Shar pointed toward the sandals and gestured we take them. I shook my head in decline, so we proceeded.

As we neared the end of the table we spotted the legs of the skeletal being who had arrived just this morning aboard his brooding, black, and silver ship. He had been greeted with great pomp and ceremony by Risan and the Council. He had been wearing a massive red cloak that hung to the ground and swirled dust with each step he took. Tonight, the bottom of that same cloak lay gathered in folds around the legs of his chair. We might have continued on, selecting a different prey, but for the memory of his disdained look at the three of us earlier, when we had run, breathlessly, into the foray of the main hall, skidding to a stop just inches from him. He was from a world that frowned on humor and youthful frivolity. He was openly vexed at three young people being allowed to scurry around unsupervised. Consequently, this made a perfect choice for this present adventure.

Slowly and ever so carefully, we crept toward his chair. Myra stealthily reached out and drew the corners of the cape so they rested beneath his chair between the legs. Then, with the swiftness of a slither, we tied the corners together, thereby guaranteeing that when the occupant of the chair rose to leave so would the chair. We quickly scurried back to the end of the table. Having accomplished our objective we modified our plan and retreated from the Great Hall to position ourselves on the balcony overlooking the banquet.

The meal continued as we watched. The servers came and cleared away the main course and the guests were then presented with desserts, delicacies, and beverages to conclude the meal.

Shortly after all had been served, we noticed a messenger arrive, whom the attendant directed toward the center of the room. The messenger quickly walked to the very guest that had been maintaining our focus. As we glanced at each other, the messenger bent and whispered in the ear of our unsuspecting victim. He nodded, then spoke quietly to my mother, Sosja, who was seated next to him. With that he quickly stood and turned, unaware of the condition of his imprisonment. The cape had indeed secured his chair and the turning chair struck the table sending it tilting toward the guests seated on the opposite side. Desserts and beverages flew. Guests screamed as they jumped to avoid the onslaught of food, they in turn upsetting the guests at the next table. This scene continued down the entire length of the Great Hall.

We had not anticipated that all of this could happen by simply tying the cape's corners together. Above the commotion we heard Risan's bellowing voice.

"Sealo! Shar! Myra! I know you are here! Show yourselves!"

Ever so slowly we rose from our hiding place. Risan's eyes were darting about the hall in search of us but, as yet, he had not looked up toward the balcony. For one brief moment we thought

The "Oh No" Trio

we might be able to escape, but those riveting eyes froze us in place. As Risan's jaw twitched, he slowly and calmly spoke. "Meet me in my quarters!"

Two

We took every detour we could think of on our way to Risan's quarters. We even stopped by the kitchen to offer our help in cleaning up the hall. The head cook informed us that he thought we had done enough 'helping' for one day. We were not sure what he meant, since he was known for his great sense of humor. We decided not to pursue the topic in view of the broken dishes being carried into the kitchen by the servers.

We continued our side track by heading straight for the Learning Center. When we had declined Risan's invitation to attend the banquet, our reason had been to study. Just at that moment Uncle Shanar was returning to the living quarters and intercepted us. He was already aware of the happenings in the Great Hall. He advised us to turn around and make haste for Risan's quarters before there were any additional consequences. Considering the look in his eyes we accepted his advice and did a quick about face and proceeded down the walkway that led to the main quarters.

Yet, speed was still the furthest thing from our minds as we trudged through the cool arboretum that surround Risan's rooms. There must be a way we could stall this uncomfortable meeting.

I looked at Shar, then Myra. They both looked as long faced as I must have. We honestly had not meant to create such a scene and disturb the important negotiations that Risan had been holding with the guest of the banquet. We knew it had taken a great deal of persuading for the Council to convince some of the star systems to attend this meeting. But, a little humor never hurt... did it?

As we approached the great doors leading to Risan's rooms, they suddenly opened. Out stormed our victim. He stopped abruptly at seeing us. His eyes shone hard obsidian black. It was obvious he was not pleased to see us. He stepped to the side as we passed but turned, never taking his eyes off his tormentors until we had cleared the portal and the doors had closed behind us.

Sosja and Ela stood talking in the anteroom. They looked up as we approached. No words were exchanged. There was really nothing we could say. Their faces softened as we passed and they reached out to touch each one of us on the head. We knew they would do anything within their power to help us, but it seemed, this time, we had over-stretched even their influence with Risan.

Slowly we opened the inner door and proceeded toward the large silver desk located at the far side of Risan's study. Placed in front of the desk were three chairs. The customary plush cushions had been removed, leaving the hard shiny surface bare and uninviting. I wondered if this was intentional.

Cautiously, Shar positioned himself on the left chair and I eased into the right one. That left the middle for Myra. Risan was no where in the room. We breathed a sign of relief. I looked to Shar, sitting straight with his feet planted firmly on the floor. What thoughts were going through his head, I wondered. Myra was squirming in her chair, her legs swinging. She was much younger than we and her small feet did not even touch the floor.

The waiting was extremely stressful. My eyes swept the room. We had been here before, on many occasions, for many reasons, but never under such dire circumstances. Risan was definitely steamed, with just cause.

Suddenly the side door opened and Risan entered. He walked slowly, coming to a stop behind his large silver desk. He leaned forward and placed his hands firmly on the smooth surface. He looked directly into our faces.

"Do you have any idea what the three of you have caused? It required many concessions on the part of the Council to even gather all the participants to this meeting. With just one of your creative adventures, you have placed all that effort in jeopardy."

"It is true our culture encourages and supports creative endeavors. It allows the young freedom to exercise their imaginations and explore new knowledge, but on many occasions you three have pushed this freedom to the limit."

"The ambassador from Kala was not amused by your experiment in containment. He was not impressed with your procedures for gaining knowledge regarding cause and effect. He has requested this household hold you accountable for the consequences of your actions." Risan said with calm restraint. "I agree with him that some amends are necessary. I'm sure you also feel this is fair. So, I would like your input as to what form these amends should take."

Typically, Risan had made the deed a learning experience and had required us to exercise some effort to correct the results of our actions. Mystified, we looked to each other in hope that some great enlightenment would occur, that would free us from this predicament. Alas, as time slowly passed, we realized that Risan would continue to wait for us to speak...even if it took hours.

I spoke first. "Perhaps we could formally apologize to all the guests? We could do this at the morning meal."

"That is, at least, a beginning," said Risan, "but, because of the magnitude of these action's effects, I feel more is required."

"Then," said Shar, "we could act as pages for the ambassador while he is here at the Complex; be ever ready to do what he needs done."

"That is a good suggestion," Risan nodded, "provided I can convince him to let you be in his presence. That may take some doing, Any other suggestions?"

Myra's small voice squeaked as she spoke. "Maybe we could be banished to a far star for the rest of the time the meeting is being conducted?"

"That might be a little too extreme, I think, but I appreciate your offer," replied Risan. "And, what are your suggestions regarding future adventures?"

The "Oh No" Trio

Quickly, the three of us answered, almost in unison, "And, in the future, we will think through all the possible effects of the plans we make, trying to see all probabilities."

"Very good," Risan said. "Now, you may go, so I can speak with the ambassador about whether he will accept your services. One other thing, you...all three of you...are confined to your quarters for the remainder of the day. Now, go."

Silently, we slipped from the chairs and crept from the room, trying to be as invisible as possible. Over my shoulder, I could have sworn, I heard a muffled chuckle come from behind the great silver desk.

Three

My quarters are warm. The light in my sleeping area is turned on and cast a cool blue glow over the iridescent mauve coverlet. The coverlet is turned back to invite the sleeper. This is Sosja's way of saying "I love you!" and "I hope everything is OK." The bed hovers above the carpeted floor like a cloud over a soft tundra. Large cylinder pillows are at each end of the five meter square surface. Across the room is a large picture window that overlooks the solarium outside the Learning Center. From here one can see the marble stairs leading to the massive front doors. Beneath the window a couch with its swirling pattern also invites this weary body. Beside the couch is a small table on which is placed my collection of miniatures. Not known as much of a collector of things, these tiny treasures invoke many memories. Each one sits pristinely on the glass top that has been polished to an almost mirror-like quality, allowing each object to reflect, thereby appearing to be two. At one end of the room my desk stands ready, piled with a variety of learning capsules we use for classes. Much information is contained in these small silver orbs. A wardrobe occupies the other end of the room and the door is slightly ajar, revealing a large array of clothing. One thing I do enjoy collecting is unusual pieces of attire from the various star systems I have visited with Risan.

As ambassador for our world, Risan travels far and has allowed me to accompany him to prepare for my future role in our society.

He has always been very tolerant. Actually, he has always been very understanding and loving. He has been the father I lost so long ago. Ah! But alas, that is a story best untold. Deep in thought, I walk to the window. The day has been a comedy of mishaps. There have been occasions almost as bad. Yet, Risan seemed overly upset with this latest adventure.

I felt something important was brewing. Never before has such a diverse group of emissaries been invited to the Complex. Usually there is a common thread that ties guests together but I can't clearly see one in this case. There is a rumor that a new alliance is being formed between Kala and another star system, but I never put much stock in rumors.

The beings of Kala are such an enigma to me. I've never been able to see how they, with their restrictive code of interaction regarding youth and humor, could truly be living in their hearts as beings of love. Risan has admonished me on several occasions about being close-minded and judgmental. This is indeed something I work on frequently. Will I ever become that tolerant being of Oneness without any disparencies toward other beings who are different. Well, I am still young and have much to learn.

Each day I am again thankful for an uncle such as Risan and an aunt such as Ela. Their loving hearts are an inspiration. They have opened their home to so many souls who have been in need of healing. Our world has been a haven and way station for many from all over this universe. The classrooms at the Learning Center are open to any who choose to enrich themselves in the ways of the One. The Healing Center has cared for numerous beings who needed our special skills and techniques. Even some one time enemies, who have tried to destroy this culture are admitted.

Risan has always believed in the miracle of love and it's ability to make right any problem. It is almost impossible to think he might ever have been young like me. Sometimes when I look into his gentle face and I feel the tenderness in his words, I know that it has taken many lifetimes of real living for him to have become so wise. Will I ever be even half as wise as Risan?

I was pulled from my reflecting by a tapping sound coming from a vent in the floor. When we left Risan's quarters earlier we had promised we would comply with his instructions. Yet, that is most certainly Shar's signal. He must have something very important to talk about to go against Risan's directions.

I reach for the vent cover and gently remove it, leaving a clear entry into the tunnel below my floor. This portion of the complex is unique in that it has a maze of caverns running beneath it. This assortment of tunnels has an opening into every room in this section.

The above ground rooms are entered through the main hallway with no interconnecting doors. They were at one time used for visiting dignitaries who preferred their privacy and protection. I'm not sure how long the caverns have been beneath the floors, probably since the original construction of the Complex. Risan's household converted the rooms to living quarters when the new Learning Center was built. The two areas so close together enable the parents of the children attending the Center to be in closer proximity.

Shar and I discovered the tunnels when we were very young and on an exploring expedition. Since then we have used them so often that the routes between our rooms are well worn, as are a few other crucial paths.

I ease myself into the tunnel and head for Shar's room.

Four

When I reached Shar's room Myra was already there sitting on one of Shar's brightly colored cushions.

"This had better be very important!" I said, as I crawled from the tunnel. "We promised Risan we would spend this time pondering our actions."

"That is exactly what we are going to do," responded Shar, with a smile. "Ponder our actions."

"I was referring to past actions," I replied. "By the spark in your eyes you are looking ahead to future actions. Am I right?"

"Correct," Shar admitted. "Myra and I have been trying to think of a way to make up to Risan for all the stress we caused today. We have come upon an idea."

"I'll listen, but I'm not so sure we should do anything. It appears we've done plenty already. Besides, most of the ideas we have come up with lately have backfired and created more than just embarrassment," I said.

"We know that," replied Myra, "so this idea is meant to create a little joy in Risan's life. It's especially for him, to show him how sorry we are for what happened."

"So what is this idea?" I asked.

"Well," continued Myra, "you know that we have no animals here, but some systems do. Some of these animals are treated as pets by beings in those systems. The pets give love, joy, and companionship. We thought it might be nice for Risan to have a pet, to bring him joy and be his companion. What do you think?"

"Explain further and I'll let you know. You realize our culture holds the belief that every being deserves to live free. Controlling another life force would go against that belief and not be tolerated." I replied.

"Yes, we know. That is why our idea is so terrific," said Shar. "This pet would not be a living thing. It would be a droid and respond telepathically. That way it could be programmed to hear only what Risan was requesting."

"And, what would this pet look like?" I asked.

"It would be soft with fur of a bright orange," responded Myra, "so it could be seen easily. It should have fluffy ears that are secured to each side of its head. This is where we could place the receivers. It should be about twenty centimeters long, so it would fit comfortably on Risan's lap. It should move on air, hover, so it could travel over any terrain. It should have two bright blue eyes in its face -- round, I think -- that give off a soft glow. What do you think?"

"Actually, it sounds very nice. We'll need materials to build it." I said.

"I've already started to work on that part," said Shar, as he returned from the far end of the room. "Here's some orange furry material we can use for the outside. I got it from another star system I visited once."

"OK. Myra, can you start drawing up the design? I'll get to work on the program for the telepathy. We will need a copy of Risan's thought voice so we can feed it into the program. Once we have a design we can begin construction. This might work out very nicely. What a terrific idea."

"Now we had better split and get back to our own rooms before it is discovered we are missing." I said. "We can talk more tomorrow."

Quietly I slipped back into the tunnel and made my way back to my room. As I ascended through the vent into the room I knew instantly that something was amiss. Someone had come in while I was gone. It appeared that I had some more explaining to do. I

The "Oh No" Trio

could tell by the energy that my visitor had been Risan. Great, now how do I get out of this one. Good intentions gone sideways again.

Five

Having had a very restless night, I awoke with a start. There was a presence in my room. I checked to see if Risan had returned to talk, but saw no one. Still the energy persisted.

I arose and began preparing for the day. I hope today goes better than yesterday, I thought. Of course anything would be an improvement over those disastrous events. Even remembering caused me to shudder. How could so much have happened because of one simple act?

Today there was to be a tour of the Complex for the visiting ambassadors. The mid-day meal was to be served outdoors on the meadow. Then the meetings would begin in the Great Hall. I thought back at the presence of Risan's energy in my quarters last evening, when I returned from Shar's room and decided maybe I should visit my uncle before his day began.

I hastily finished my morning preparations and let myself out into the main hallway. All was quiet. No one seemed to be about yet. I hurried in the direction of Risan's quarters and was just about to knock when I heard my name whispered.

I turned searching for the source. The sound had come from across the hall. There a corridor led off from the main hallway directly to the dining area. There standing in the shadows was Shar. He was motioning for me to come. I turned and walked toward him while holding my hand over my mouth as a signal for silence.

The "Oh No" Trio

Together we moved quickly down the passageway stopping a safe distance from Risan's room.

"What do you want?" I asked.

"Were you called by Risan?" replied Shar. "I was surprised to see you heading for his quarters so early."

I explained to Shar about Risan's energy in my room last night and said I had decided to follow up on it before I was summoned.

"Do you think it was important?" Shar asked.

"I'm not sure but I would like to find out. By the way, how is our little project coming along? Were you able to get the materials we need?" I inquired.

Shar had always been the procurer when any of our ideas required special items. Not that we needed an agent...any of us could manifest what we needed just by thinking it. But, Shar's method of securing always reaped such wonderful and unusual pieces...things we never dreamed existed. That is one of his special talents -- producing what we need when we need it.

"Yes, we now have most of what we need for the project." he replied. "Myra has finished the design and we can begin construction. But, how are we going to get a print of Risan's thought waves to do the programming?"

"I was hoping to get that at the same time I find out about his visit last night. I brought one of the knowledge orbs from the Learning Center with me. I already have it set on receive so I can record his brain patterns. I feel a little nervous about being so secretive but we do want this to be a grand surprise. I'm sure he won't be upset." I said.

"I hope you're right," Shar replied. "We wouldn't want any more *consequences* to make amends for."

"We can meet later in your room to work on the project," I said. "Now I want to catch Risan before anyone else secures his attention."

I quickly turned to Risan's doors and knocked. From inside I heard his voice call, "Enter!".

The doors between the anteroom and his study stood open. I could see him sitting behind his great silver desk. Ela was at his side and they were discussing some items that were laying on the shiny surface.

I slowly entered the room. Risan lifted his head, motioned me forward, at the same time, speaking quietly to Ela. My aunt smiled at me, then turned and left the room.

Risan looked straight at me and asked, "Yes?"

"Last night I felt your presence in my room," I stated. "I thought it best if I came to you first thing to talk."

"Very good choice," he said. "Yes, I was there, but you were evidently on some very important task that made it necessary for you to challenge my instructions."

"Ahhh!" I started.

Risan lifted his hand to quiet me. "We can discuss this later. Right now I have these meetings to concentrate on and they are very important. The reason for my visit last nigh --- I talked with the Kalan representative and he has declined your offer to be pages for him. He has his own aides who came here with him. He prefers I assign you to some other task that will keep you out of his vicinity while he is at the Complex. I suspected that might be the case, so I have asked Ela and Sosja to keep you occupied. The three of you are to do as they request and stay out of mischief. Understand?"

"Yes," I replied. "We really are very sorry, Uncle. We did not mean to cause such problems."

"I know, things just seem to happen when the three of you are together. That has always been the case. Now is there anything else you wish to speak to me about?"

"No," I said. "Thank you. May I go now?"

"Yes," he replied.

As I left his quarters I began to question the wisdom of this latest project. Maybe...

Just at that time Shar joined me in the hallway.

"Is everything all right?", he asked.

"I think so. The Kalan representative doesn't wish to have us as his pages. He has requested that we be occupied far away from him, so Risan has put Ela and Sosja in charge of us till the meetings are

The "Oh No" Trio

finished. We'll have to postpone working on our gift for Risan till these gatherings are over. Let's go get Myra and then go see what Ela and Sosja have for us to do."

Six

We found Ela and Sosja at the edge of the meadow. They were preparing the area for the mid-day meal. Large tables were arranged in rows. An oval table commanded a spot by the pond where the food would be placed.

Lovely flowers were being carried in to decorate as centerpieces and standards. The fragrance from the flowers filled the air with such sweetness it made your heart soar.

Surely, Ela and Sosja knew what the Kalan representative had requested. To have us working around the meal place would not be to his liking.

As we walked toward them, a flash of light crossed our vision. It appeared to come from the top of one of the small hills that borders the meadow. Looking more carefully we realized it was being made by light reflecting off a mirror like metallic material hidden somewhere in the grass above us. We then noticed several figures moving about. That's right! There was to be entertainment after the meal and those workers must be constructing the platform for the musicians. The guests would be seated on the sloping hillside in the grass.

Ela and Sosja motioned us toward the platform. By their signal it was clear that was where we were to help. Slowly we climbed the hill. This definitely would separate us from the happenings in the meadow.

The "Oh No" Trio

The platform was only half finished. The foundation struts still needed to be put into place. Droids were lifting the heavy pieces into place so they could be secured.

We approached the one we thought was directing the activities and inquired about our duties. She showed us to the far end of the platform. The stairs were located at this end of the platform and our job was to assist the musicians in climbing up the stairs with their equipment. The task seemed to be simple enough and allowed us time to explore until the platform was complete and the musicians arrived.

We moved on up the hill a bit. The day was warm with just a slight breeze. We decided to lie down in the cool, sweet grass and relax until we were needed. We discussed the project and how we hoped Risan would enjoy his pet. As the time moved lazily on we grew drowsy and fell asleep.

The sound of voices in the meadow below woke us. The midday meal was in progress. The guests were all seated and the servers were delivering the food and beverages. We had slept longer than we thought.

We looked around for the director of the platform assignment, but it appeared that everyone had returned to the Complex. Probably they were needed to help the entertainers bring their equipment up. The platform stood shining in the daylight. The side plates were decorated with the many geometric symbols representing the various members of the gathering. The grass on the side of the hill waived gently as a light wind moved down the slope into the meadow.

Someone laughed from below. We stretched to see if we could identify who it might be, but we were not tall enough. We knew these were the same guests that had attended last evenings banquet. From where we stood we could not get a clear view of the area below. If we climbed on to the platform we could see all the happenings. Even though the stairs were not in place and the platform was a good seven meters high, we felt we could make the climb.

The platform creaked a little as Shar lifted me up. We figured it was just settling and we would be fine. Then we reached back for Myra. As we pulled her onto the floor beside us the platform began to creak even more loudly. Standing and placing her securely between the two of us, we carefully worked our way toward the front of the platform. The view would be best from there since it looked out over the area at the foot of the hill. As we neared the edge, the flat surface we had been walking across began to tilt slightly. We froze in place hoping that things would settle. But, the platform continued to move...to lean... toward the sloping hillside... toward the meadow below.

At that very moment, the members of the construction crew arrived carrying large metal beams. They were hollering at us.

"The platform is unstable. The main supports have not been braced!"

Boy, they didn't need to tell us. We were standing on a surface that was steadily leaning farther and farther. We scrambled to lay face down, so we could ease over the floor to the back of the platform. But, the slanting hillside was successfully capturing the platform. Suddenly, every metal plate and beam that had been the platform collapsed with an explosive sound and began to slide down the hill.

We couldn't believe what was happening. The three of us, laying face down on the metal floor, were traveling at a high rate of speed... down the hillside...to the meadow below...straight toward the tables full of guests and food... and there was nothing we could do to stop.

We heard shouting from below and could hear the clamor of moving bodies above the crashing of chairs. The platform hit the tables with the force of an exploding rocket. Food flew everywhere. Shar, Myra, and I were covered with runny, sticky globs.

The platform slowed, having spent the momentum of its downhill slide, and came to a stop on the flat surface of the meadow. We looked at each other in relief that we were still in one piece.

But, our relief was short lived when we realized we would probably be better off dead than in our present position. For there, standing just at the edge of the destroyed platform was Risan, covered with food. Standing beside him, likewise decorated, was the Kalan Ambassador.

Seven

"But Uncle Risan, this time it was an accident. We didn't do anything. The platform just collapsed," I explained, as I moved out to the edge of my chair opposite the great silver desk in Risan's study.

Shar and Myra sat very straight in their regular chairs. This time there were more than three chairs clustered in front of Risan's desk. Ela and Sosja occupied two, one on each side of us. The Kalan ambassador and Uncle Shanar were seated in chairs that flanked each side of the desk. We had already apologized profusely to the ambassador, but the apology was not well taken. So, we were here, in the study, to determine the next course of action.

Uncle Shanar was present because he, more or less, oversaw our studies and regardless of what the others decided our education would continue in a somewhat structured fashion.

The silence hung heavy all around us. This was a very serious situation indeed. These meetings were crucial to the well-being of many star systems who interact with the Council. Our disruptions have caused quite a commotion among the representatives. They were even questioning the wisdom of continuing the gathering at this location, casting doubt on Risan's capabilities as a leader of his household.

Risan stood up from his chair and began to pace behind the desk. "We will definitely have to separate the three of you, at least for the remainder of the gathering time. Likewise, you all need to be sent some place where you can be supervised. There is also the matter of making amends for what has occurred. Accidents do happen but you did not think through your actions, otherwise when the platform collapsed you would not have been on top of it. Similarly, the platform may not have collapsed at all if not for your weight on the unsupported beams."

"Now," he continued, "where to send you? Any suggestions? And Myra, please don't suggest a far star or this time I might just agree."

Ela spoke, "Konal is taking a fleet of ships out for our routine visits to the other stars in our system. He may be willing to add three aides to his crew. That would have them away from the Complex for one complete mooning cycle."

"I appreciate what you are suggesting, but I still feel they need to be separated, at least for a while," Risan replied. "What Ela suggested would work for Shar and Sealo but Myra is still too young for such an assignment. Any other suggestions?"

"One could go with me," said Shanar. "I'm taking a group of students into the hills for classes in Natural Healing. We will be gone for half the moon cycle. We plan to leave tomorrow."

"Myra can stay here with Ela and myself," injected Sosja. "There is plenty she can do around the Complex and with the other two gone she might be less distracted from her tasks."

"Sounds like three very workable arrangements," responded Risan. "So, Shar, you will go with Konal. Sealo, you are to go with Shanar. Myra will remain here at the Complex. Are these arrangements acceptable to you Ambassador?"

"Yes, they will do," he retorted. We got the distinct impression he was not altogether pleased by the outcome but had conceded.

Risan continued, "Shanar, be sure that Shar has enough lessons ready to take with him on this trip. We want him to maintain his progress. Assign someone from Konal's crew to oversee his studies. As for Sealo, you, yourself can monitor his lessons And we, here at the Complex will see to Myra's.

The "Oh No" Trio

"Thank you for coming, everyone. Now, I think it is time we get on with our other duties," said Risan.

As we left the room, our hearts were very heavy. This time I did not hear Risan chuckle.

Eight

Back in my room I began to prepare for the time away. This is probably for the best...going away. Everything seems sour right now. I had been meaning to take Uncle Shanar's class on Natural Healing and I guess there is no time like the present.

As I laid out the things I needed, I again felt there was a presence in the room. I could not identify the energy. It was vaguely familiar, but I couldn't pin it down. I had done some energy identification work at the Healing Center. Many beings assisted there. Some were not in physical form. We were encouraged to know the different healers by their energy. This, at times, is no easy task. There are several general groups of beings, each one giving off their own unique energy pattern. By identifying these energy patterns, then by further extending, you can begin to recognize individuals within groups. Each being has their own special vibration, temperature, and aroma.

This energy was different, almost a blend of more than one kind. That could mean it might be produced by the essence of two beings. It was not uncomfortable and it certainly didn't arouse any concern on my part. It felt very loving and supportive.

A tap on the door brought me out of my pondering. Who could be calling on me? After a day like today I was almost tempted to not answer.

The "Oh No" Trio

Opening the door I was truly surprised to find Shar and Myra standing at my threshold, looking acutely nervous.

Glancing quickly from side to side, Shar whispered, "Well, can we come in?"

"Yes, of course," I said. "This might be the last chance we can meet...at least for a while, anyway."

As I pushed back the door they entered. Myra was carrying that bright orange fur tightly against her chest. I checked the hallway and closed the door. When I turned she was standing in the middle of the room, arms outstretched, with that bit of fluff clutched in her small hands.

"I finished it," she said, with delight and her face beaming. "The only thing left to do is program it. We thought we might leave it for Risan as a way of saying we are sorry."

"Do you think you could program it tonight?" asked Shar. "Do you still have Risan's thought prints."

I quickly retrieved the silver orb with Risan's pattern from my desk. I had placed it there when I returned this morning. That seems so long ago. "Here," I said. "We should be able to do this easily enough. We will simply imprint the receiver in the pet with Risan's thought pattern. This way it will respond only to his directions. Now, we'll put in a blocker to be sure it will not mistakenly answer someone else's thought directions. The blocker is a simple metal shaving that can be placed into the outer shell of the receiver, here, in the ear." As I spoke I inserted the blocker into the pet's receiver. "There, it is ready to be presented to Risan."

"Maybe we better not give it to him personally," said Shar. "I don't think he really wants to see us right now. Let's just place it in his quarters and leave him a message that will activate the pet."

"That's probably best," I agreed. "What should the message say?"

"How about a poem?" asked Myra. "That way he will know how we feel."

Shar and I concurred. This would be a good way to handle it. We began composing the poem, hoping to express how we felt about what had happened over the past few days.

J.L. Alonzo

A short time later we slipped silently into the hallway and headed toward Risan's quarters. Our priceless present was lying safely on a very special bed we had made so Risan would have a place to keep his new pet.

Risan always spent this time of evening with Ela in the nursery, settling the young for their rest time. We knew this would give us time to place our surprise in his room.

A soft glow of pleasure washed over us as we crept quietly into the anti-room of Risan's quarters. The door to his sleeping area lay to the right and it was our intent to place his new friend beneath his bed, to be summoned when Risan read the poem. We hoped it would pleasantly surprise him. We completed the placement quickly, careful not to disturb anything and give away the surprise. We then placed the poem on his pillow so he could find it easily. How we wished we could be there to see his face at this wonderful present. Myra promised to give Shar and me a complete accounting when we returned.

Our task finished, we slipped out of the room and softly into the hallway, retracing our steps to my room. We bid each other farewell at my door. Shar and Myra hurried on down the hall to their sleeping areas.

As I closed the door behind me I smiled, thinking of the pleasure Risan will feel knowing he is so loved. I sure hope this helps make things brighter for all of us.

Nine

I woke at the appointed time and felt a tingle seep through my body as I donned the outfit I had selected for this outing. I really was looking forward to some time away from the Complex. Things had become so complicated lately. So many good ideas had gone sour.

Uncle Shanar had issued each student a list of items needed for the class. Since most of us were just beginning to develop the skill of manifesting it was sometimes necessary for us to actually carry things with us. What we needed was usually manifested by a family member to be used by the young during their schooling.

The weather is never an issue on Astara for the temperature remains constant at twenty seven degrees Celsius and there are never any unusual weather patterns to deal with. It is always light on Astara since it is a star and has no sun. What we call moons are really two smaller stars that orbit in the stratosphere above us. They have a definite pattern or cycle and this is how we tell time. Some planets in our galaxy have moons. These moons move faster than our star satellites. Also, on these planets, that get their light from a central sun, the moons have phases going from fully illuminated to totally darkened because of the blocking effect of the planet. Here we have no phases. We count time by the moons' full orbit around our star broken into increments we call days.

This trip is to last one-half of a moon cycle and will take us many kilometers away from the Complex. Uncle Shanar has taken many

J.L. Alonzo

such groups out and from all reports the students have always been able to acquire a wealth of knowledge.

I, personally, am looking forward to some peace and serenity after the terrible ordeals of these past few days. I always enjoy delving into some new topic and derive great satisfaction from learning something new.

I picked up my pack and proceeded to check my room for anything forgotten or amiss. As I reached for the latch on the door I again felt that wonderful energy. It felt as though I were being wrapped in a loving embrace. It is as if someone were wishing me farewell and good luck while at the same time screaming don't leave me.

Exiting my door I came face to face with the Kalan Ambassador. He was coming down the hallway at a rather fast pace and if I had not dodged to the side he would have run into me. I looked quickly in the direction from which he had come. I saw Risan standing outside the doors to his quarters. He looked tired and pensive, like he may have just completed a rather lengthy and exhausting meeting. My guess is he had not even entered his sleeping room since yesterday morning. At the look of tiredness on his face, I was again glad we had made him such a delightful surprise.

I hurried down the hallway toward the exit that led to the Learning Center. I did not want to be late and cause the others to delay their departure. As I cleared the doorway and started down the stairs I could see Uncle Shanar at a distance. Gathered around him were probably ten students roughly my age, maybe a little older. There was a sense of excitement and anticipation in the air. This is indeed going to be a wonderful experience and everyone was anxious to be on their way.

I caught up with the group just as they started to walk away from the Complex. I hurried to Shanar's side and smiled. He nodded, then returned his attention to the path we were following. I fell back to walk beside one of the other students.

"I'm really excited about taking this class. How about you? I've heard wonderful things about it. I understand we will be learning

The "Oh No" Trio

about some great healing techniques." I was rambling hoping to strike up a friendship.

Abruptly Shanar turned to me and, though his voice was calm and smooth, I could tell he was not particularly pleased with my behavior. "Since you missed the initial introductions, you should know that these first two kilometers are to be a time of silence and observation. We will stop up the way and I will be asking each student to give a description of what they have seen. This is a class and I'll expect you to adhere to the guidelines outlined in the preview I sent to each student. I sent one to your quarters, but evidently you neglected to listen to yours." With that, he placed a learning orb in my hand and turned around. He proceeded down the path leaving me red-faced and stunned.

I looked down at the silver orb. The markings struck a cord in my memory, but I was so flustered right now I couldn't think. I cupped the orb in my hand and listened to the instructions. The first voice I heard was Risan telling about the class and expounding on its virtues. Then Uncle Shanar spoke. Then a variety of other speakers talked about natural healing and how it is used within our culture. There were many very visual descriptions of the kinds of life forms we would encounter. All in all, there was probably the voice of everyone at the Learning Center, the Healing Center and quite a few from the Complex's living area.

As I more closely examined the orb I realized it was an exact replica of the orb I had retrieved from my desk last night. *Realization hit with a jolt!* I had programmed Risan's pet with the thought patterns of everyone in the instructional orb and with or without the blocker, the pet would respond to just about everyone in the Complex.

Looking remorsefully back down the path, I thought, Oh no! Here we go again!"

Ten

The countryside was quiet and fragrant as we walked single file down the path. Uncle Shanar led the way. There were so many things to remember: the colors, the smells, the sounds. We were expected to see and feel things we didn't normally notice. Uncle Shanar would be asking many questions and I needed to be prepared.

I tried very hard to concentrate but my mind kept returning to the Complex, wondering if Risan had found his pet...or had someone else caused the pet to come to life and what had been the results. I felt sorry that Myra would have to face the situation alone.

I need to keep my mind in this class! If not, there will be more consequences. Uncle Risan has had such a turbulent time lately. I'm sure he would like very much for his life to calm down.

The voices of my companions brought me back from my pondering. Coming toward us, down the path, was a party of four young people. They looked as if they had been traveling for quite some time. Their attire was mussed and there was a tiredness in their gait. I did not recognize the markings on their clothing. Yet, there are many settlements in this region around the Complex. They may be from one of these. Each settlement has distinct geometric symbols that identify the members of the community. I have not ventured very far from the Complex because of my busy schedule with schooling and my travels with Uncle Risan.

The "Oh No" Trio

I remember once when I was quite young, my mother and Aunt Ela visited one of the outlying settlements and had taken Shar and I with them. I can still recall how differently the people of the settlement lived. Each family had their own individual living area where they slept and ate. These were dwellings clustered around a large central building. This building had a small Learning Center, a Healing Center, a Laboratory, a small Temple, and a very large meeting area. The people of the settlement gathered in this meeting area to make decisions about matters that affected everyone. Each settlement is devoted to a specialized focus that is part of the whole system within the kingdom. This settlement's main function was the development and growing of natural healing herbs. These herbs were harvested and distributed throughout the system or anywhere else they were needed. Sometimes entire plants were sent to other worlds so the herbs could be cultivated there and those cultures could become self-sustaining.

My mother is very involved with this part of our world's activities. At the Complex she oversees the development of Natural Healers. As such, sometimes it is necessary for her to travel to settlements to see if any new discoveries have occurred. Aunt Ela will occasionally accompany her because they are very close. It amazes me that Aunt Ela is able to find the time to get away. She oversees the main nursery at the Complex and this consumes a great deal of her time and energy.

I remember the feeling of openness I felt as I strolled through the settlement. It was nothing like the massive solids of the Complex with its large buildings. I enjoyed the feeling very much. It was like the feeling I get when I travel with Uncle Risan in space.

I startled as Uncle Shanar's voice broke through my thoughts. "Sealo! Sealo?" he said, with a touch of impatience. "I'd like to introduce you to someone."

"Yes, Uncle Shanar," I replied.

He led me toward the four newcomers. By their actions I felt they were well acquainted with Uncle Shanar. He smiled as he greeted them. They returned his greeting and began eagerly talking to him, telling him of their adventures.

J.L. Alonzo

I stood there mesmerized. She was the most beautiful being I had ever seen. I could not take my eyes off her. Her movements were graceful and her voice was a warm floating music that sent a wonderful tingling throughout my entire body. I was lost in a cloud of her essence. She continued talking with the others but her eyes kept darting in my direction.

Just then, Uncle Shanar motioned for me to come forward. I felt incapable of movement. My legs went numb and my feet would not respond. Finally, I was able to regain some control and proceeded slowly toward the five of them, my eyes still holding her focus.

"This is my nephew, Sealo. He is a member of this latest Natural Healing class. You will be studying under his mother's supervision." Uncle Shanar said to the four of them.

Turning to me he continued, "Sealo, these are some of our finest budding Natural Healers that live in the settlement you visited with your mother when you were younger."

He began to introduce them but I heard only the first one.

"This is Ulena, daughter of the settlement's Sage. She is coming to the Complex to study. And this is..."

She is headed for the Complex...to study...to stay. My heart leapt in my chest. I smiled and said hello. Then I stumbled at finding something else to say to this divine being. I was truly speechless. How embarrassing. I should come up with something marvelous and witty so she would remember me but my mind had turned to mush.

Uncle Shanar concluded the introductions, made a few more comments about seeing them later at the Complex, and waved them good-bye as they started on their way. He glanced at me, grinned, then turned and began striding up the path away from them...away from the Complex.

This is going to make this half cycle even more intolerable. Here I am exiled to the countryside and now my heart has left me and is traveling with Ulena toward the Complex.

ELEVEN

Focus! Focus! But, my mind keeps returning to the Complex. Agony and ecstasy! I wanted so badly to return...to help unravel the mess I was sure surrounded the pet's appearance into Risan's life and to pursue a relationship, I was even more sure, had been conceived by the greatest loves of the universe.

Time passed in a haze. I cannot even remember a time when I was not interested in a course of studies. This was definitely a first. I usually thrived on the learning process and yet, this time, I was withering away. Uncle Shanar showed his concern by not singling me out to perform as often as he usually did. Since I excelled in scholastics I had often been the example. Ah! Not this time.

Gratefully the time did pass and, finally, we were again on the path leading toward the Complex. With each step my heart became lighter and at the same time my anxiety grew. What awaited me on my return I could only imagine and these thoughts were not pleasant.

At a distance we could see the beautiful shining top of the pyramid that was in the center of the Temple. This had always been the first landmark that all visitors saw to let them know they were almost to their destination.

My heart leapt. Soon...very soon...I would discover the truth about what happened during my absence. My mind flew to Myra. I hope she had fared well. Then, as if by magic, she appeared, running toward us down the path. Her face was flushed and she was breathing fast. Never slowing, she ran head long into my arms. She gave me the strongest hug her little arms could impart...little sister greeting big brother. The big brother who had deserted her and left her alone to face... who knew what?

Instantly she began babbling. She seemed to be trying to tell me everything at once. It all came out a blur. As she fell into step beside me her breathing returned too normal, as did her speech.

I looked at her tenderly and said, "Wait! Let's go over to the meadow where we can sit down. Then you may tell me all that has happened."

We separated from the rest of the group and made our way to the meadow. When we were seated by the pond she began. This is what I heard:

"The morning you left the Complex, you saw Risan standing in the hallway outside his quarters, right? The Kalan Ambassador had just left him. They had been in a very heavy conference all night. Very weary, Risan had returned to his sleeping room to rest a bit before beginning the day.

Seeing the note on his pillow, he picked it up and read it. He was delighted by our gesture of love and caring.

He began looking for the pet but was unable to find it. He looked everywhere in his quarters. But, no pet.

It seems one of the instructors from the Learning Center had delivered a new training orb to Risan's quarters so it could be reviewed before it was used. This was sometime while Risan was still with the Kalan Ambassador. Somehow the pet responded to the thought pattern of the instructor and had followed the instructor out of Risan's room. The pet returned to the Learning Center with the instructor. This instructor was going to do some more work before classes began. When the instructor went into his teaching area the pet followed his thought path. The instructor teaches in the alchemy lab and when the pet smelled all those different and strange chemicals it must have malfunctioned. The pet began sniffing everything in sight. It got up onto the lab tables and turned over chemicals everywhere.

The instructor, never having seen such a creature, was startled and jumped backward...dislodging one of the dividers between the classrooms. The divider crashed into a display case in the next classroom. The display case was filled with valuable artifacts from another star system that were being used as part of a lesson. Thank goodness no one was in the classroom, but the artifacts were completely destroyed. The pet was traveling at a very high rate of speed, so the instructor was unable to catch it.

The pet left the lab and ran into the courtyard outside the Learning Center. One of the household staff was resting on a bench beside the pool. The pet jumped right up on her lap. The sudden movement caused the bench to tip over, dumping her and the pet into the water. As she screamed, the pet floated into the air over her head and, dripping water everywhere, scurried away into the living quarters. The staff were preparing for the morning meal and when this wet orange fluffy thing appeared, the entire place turned into chaos. One member of the staff was making bread and as the pet jumped onto the counter the flour was upset, sending a fine shower of white powder all over the room, covering the staff and the pet. The pet flew down the counter, upsetting pans, bowls, and anything else that was in its way. It escaped into the hallway, leaving a white trail in its wake.

It made its way to the Great Hall, where the tables were sitting ready for the morning meal. It was still sniffing at everything. We could tell by the nose prints on the table cloths. It traveled over every table in the hall. As it leapt from table to table, some of the cloths caught on its feet and were dragged from the tables.

It left the Great Hall and went down the corridor into the living quarters. It entered Risan's room just as Risan, who had given up looking for it, walked from his dressing room to his sleeping pad. I guess the pet thought it could make it back to it's mat under Risan's bed but Risan stepped on it just as it started under.

This caused Risan to fall and startled the pet who began spinning around very fast, all over Risan's room, upsetting everything.

Finally, Risan was able to catch it and told it to stop. The pet instantly obeyed and went right to sleep in Risan's arms.

J.L. Alonzo

Shock waves surged through me as I sat listening to the unfolding drama...an act of love gone crazy. Compassionately, I looked at Myra as she finished her tale. To think it all happened the very morning I left. I was still at the Complex. It's unbelievable that someone didn't stop me from leaving, to deal with the carnage. I smiled at Myra. She is such a brave little soul.

Twelve

"What happened next?" I asked. "What did Risan do?"

She swallowed hard, then continued. "He was, of course, very upset. Another fiasco for the guests that he would have to deal with. The kitchen staff had already started to renovate the Great Hall when he arrived there to survey the damages. The soiled table cloths had been removed and the staff were manifesting new ones. This was not how the Council had wanted things to be handled, but it was necessary to prevent any additional crisis. Likewise, the morning meal was manifested and served as scheduled."

As for myself, Risan summoned me right after the meal had been completed. It was very scary and lonely, sitting in his big office all by myself. If Risan was angry it did not show when he talked to me...and he did talk...for a very long time. Then he said we would talk again when you and Shar had returned.

I was kept very busy after that and never left by myself. I never saw the pet. I don't know what happened to it. I didn't ask. I thought that was best.

With that she seemed to relax a little. It must have been quite an ordeal for her. At least, now, I'm back and I might be able to release some of the pressure she has been under.

We rose and slowly started walking toward the Complex. Typically, she was again light hearted and bubbly, as if nothing unpleasant had happened and everything was rosy for the future. At this moment she seemed very content walking beside her big brother. She was asking a million questions: Where have you been? What did you do? What did you see that was different and exciting? How I wished to be as young as she and so residual. But, even when I was her age I never was the bubbly type. I always have had a rather subdued, serious way about me.

I was pulled from my thoughts by someone calling my name. Shar! So the tenacious trio was once again united. As Shar briskly covered the distance between us, I wondered what lay ahead for three well meaning adventurers.

"I just returned," Shar said, as he caught up to us. "I was very surprised by the cool reception I received. I thought I'd be seeing lots of smiling faces. Instead, all I got were stern looks of reproach. What happened while I was away?"

Myra and I exchanged a look of knowing, but raised our hands, and in unison said, "Nothing very exciting."

Wrapping my arm around Shar's shoulder and grabbing Myra's hand, I turned us toward the Complex. "We'll fill you in on the way. Risan sent a message that I was to see him as soon as I returned. I wouldn't dream of visiting him alone, now that my two best friends in the whole universe are here to accompany me."

Shar shot me a quick glance and beneath my arm I felt a shudder travel through his body.

By the time we reached the steps of the living quarters, the complete story had been retold. I found myself virtually dragging Shar and Myra with me into the building. Both had expressed a strong desire to run and hide, but I convinced them that there was safety in numbers. If we faced Risan as a united front the story was less apt to be misdelivered.

An extreme silence echoed through the halls as we made our way to Risan's quarters. The living area was all but deserted, which was understandable for this time of day. I held a secret hope that we would arrive and find Risan out and about, seeing to one of his many responsibilities. Alas, as we crossed the anteroom, the door to his office swung serenely open and Ela exited. With a slightly startled expression, she motioned us toward a couch. She then re-entered

The "Oh No" Trio

Risan's office. I glanced toward Shar, indicating by my expression, I completely understood his remark about the cool reception he had received. Something was definitely amiss. I couldn't believe, after all the time that had passed since the incident with the pet, that this climate was the result of that one act.

Within moments the office door burst open revealing Risan. His feet were planted firmly and his hands were on his hips. He looked intently at the three of us. Without a word he signaled us to follow as he swept across the anteroom and headed down the hall toward the staircase that led to the upper level.

Hustling to keep up, we were at a loss to explain his actions. He continued at a rapid pace till he reached the solarium located at the end of the building that overlooked the steps to the Learning Center. He pushed the door wide for us to enter ahead of him. His silence was more terrifying than his bellowing. He motioned us toward a small alcove that contained three desks. Once we had seated ourselves, he began to pace around us, shaking his head and pulling at his lower lip. Finally he stopped, faced us, and just stood there looking at us.

This was really serious. Time slowly ticked by as we waited for what fate, through Risan, would throw our way. After an extremity period of time, he spoke.

"We cannot have any more disturbances such as the one caused by that small creature the three of you invented. You will be confined to the living quarters, *specifically these desks*, during your waking hours. You may sleep in your own rooms but you will not be permitted to take your meals in the main dining area. All that you need will be brought to you here. There will be someone with you at all times to supervise your activities. These arrangements will stand until I tell you otherwise. Is this understood?"

Shocked beyond words, we could only nod in acknowledgment. At that, Risan abruptly turned and left the room. We sat there in stunned silence for quite some time, maybe hoping to wake up from this horrible nightmare.

Thirteen

Slowly we came out of our startled state and glanced at each other. What was this all about? It had to be more than just the consequences of a few misadventures by three children. We had never seen Risan in such a disposition. Shar and I looked toward Myra.

"Tell us everything about what has been happening at the Complex while we were away."

"Well," she began, "I've already told you about the pet and Risan's talk with me. The rest of the time they kept me very busy in the Nursery or at the Learning Center. I did notice that Ela was constantly coming and going from her duties at the Nursery. I was not able to find out where these trips took her. There were a lot of beings visiting the Complex…even some species I have never seen before. I noticed them mainly at meal times and they were always seated at the head table with Risan. I was never able to get close to them because there was always someone with me. The Kalan Ambassador was here several times and that strange Bird Being. They were always talking in such hushed tones I couldn't even eavesdrop. I'm sorry I can't be of more help. Oh, one thing I did notice. There was a lot of activity at the Healing Center. I saw many beings brought in…some very seriously hurt…but I was always given some task that took me to the opposite end of the Complex when they were arriving."

The "Oh No" Trio

"That's not unusual," I commented, "our healers are the best in the galaxy and our Center is the most complete. We always have beings arriving and leaving."

"No, this was more. There were large ships full of them unloaded many times during the day...for several days," she continued. "Do you think there has been a battle somewhere?"

"There's only one way of finding out," Shar injected. "Investigate! But that might be very difficult with our restricted arrangements."

"We *can* go to our quarters and there are always the tunnels," I remarked. "But for the time being we had better stay put. I'm sure they will be watching us to see if we comply with Risan's directives."

So we settled into a routine of studying, eating, and sleeping. From time to time Risan, Ela, or Sosja would stop in to see how we were doing. They seemed pleased that we were behaving, following the orders we had been given.

As time went by the restrictions became more and more unbearable. We were used to using our imaginations and creative energy and this imposed confinement was not giving that energy an outlet.

One afternoon when the instructional material was exceptionally dry and the solarium tremendously warm, we decided to take a break and sit by the window to catch some of the fresh breeze that was rustling through the trees next to the building. Upon opening the window we were delighted to discover the sound of voices drifting up from the steps below. Evidently Uncle Shanar had also decided to take advantage of the pleasant weather. He had gathered his class on the steps and was conducting his instruction there.

It so happened we had just completed a science lesson about gravity and it's effect on objects of different weights. The kit for the experiment still sat by the door to the solarium and in an instant the ideas began to bubble. What happened to plastic spheres filled with liquid when dropped from the height of a second story window to the surface below? Could you control the direction on the descent? Could you predict how large an area would be affected by the

J.L. Alonzo

changing volume of liquid. Would that factor change the rate of descent or directional control?

We retrieved the storage box and began to fill the plastic spheres with liquid. We measured the liquid, putting different amounts in each sphere. We arranged the spheres carefully along the window sill. We decided to keep notes regarding each sphere...we noted the amount of liquid, the weight, and measurements when filled. Later we'd measure the height from the window from each step so we could use that information in the final calculations. When everything was prepared we were so excited we could hardly contain ourselves.

As a cross reference we decided to start the experiment by dropping items that were lighter than the spheres. We also decided since this was a joint experiment we would alternate taking turns. Myra was first and she choose a feather. It floated effortlessly down, was caught by the breeze and missed the steps completely. Shar was next and he selected a silk scarf. He was going to try to direct it to a particular target...an exceptionally attractive female student seated on the top step. As the scarf descended we held our breaths. It slowly fluttered downward and gently landed in the girl's lap. "Bravo, Shar! Good shot!" Another factor we were checking was the elapse time of decent. We noted the times of the two trials in our notes. I chose a cloth napkin left from our meal. My target was the student sitting next to Shar's target, only one step down. When released the napkin fell twice as fast as the scarf. We noted the difference.

By this time the students had noticed us on our perch and smiled at the little presents they had received. It was time to start releasing the spheres. We started with the lightest and would work our way up to the heaviest. As the spheres with liquid began to connect with their targets, from below squeals and laughter bubbled up. The students were delighted with the distraction from their studies and excited at the entertaining and refreshing splash. All was going well and the spheres were hitting their anticipated targets. Then we had a slight miscalculation. This error caused one of the larger spheres to find it's mark right on top of Uncle Shanar's head. Suddenly there was a deafening silence. Curiously we peered over the window sill

The "Oh No" Trio

to see Uncle Shanar standing, face uplifted, eyes like glass, water dripping from his chin.

Maybe we had pushed this experiment a little too far, but before we could utter an apology, Uncle Shanar had disappeared through the living quarters' door and we knew we were in big trouble.

Desperately we searched the solarium for a place to hide, but sufficient cover could not be found. So Shar and I called on one of the skills we had but were cautioned about using. We quickly changed our shape becoming leisure chairs beside the wall farthest from the door. Alas, poor Myra. She was not schooled in this technique and as Shanar came bursting through the door, she was the sole scientist visible in the room.

Fourteen

Restricted to our sleeping quarters! We were only conducting a science experiment. My head pounded with thoughts protesting my predicament. So what if it got a little out of control. So what if we used a skill we'd been taught to use only for protection in dire circumstances and extreme danger. There was no telling what Uncle Shanar would do when he was that perturbed. So what…oh…that we left Myra to face the consequences alone…again. Uncle Risan was right! That was totally unthinkable. We were acting irresponsibly and uncaring toward another being who looked up to us and felt safe with us. We had broken that trust.

My mind just wouldn't rest. I kept retracing the events and with each replay it became more and more contemptuous. What had I been thinking? There were many spots along the way where we could have made different choices, that wouldn't have ended in a fiasco. Of course, Uncle Shanar could detect us, even in our disguises. He knows our energy and even in shape-shifting a being's original energy vibration is detectable. Actually, it is even more discernible because of the high level of concentration needed to maintain the new shape. Boy, were we foolish!

If I don't stop pacing, there will be a hole in this beautiful rug on my floor. But, I can't seem to get my mind to relax. I hope Shar and Myra are faring better.

The "Oh No" Trio

As if my very thoughts had manifested before me, Shar and Myra emerged from the tunnel vent...fingers over their lips to indicate silence.

"They actually have guards outside our doors," Shar whispered. "I don't understand. They've never reacted this sternly before. Something very important must be in the mill for their tolerance level to be so low."

"It's time we get to the bottom of this!" I responded. "A little investigating...a fact finding mission. Myra, you said there had been a lot of traffic into and out of the Healing Center. Had there been any other areas in the Complex they kept you away from?"

A thoughtful smile crossed her face. "Yes," she said. "There were strange sentries stationed at the hallway leading to the wing on the far side of the Great Hall. Many servants bustled in and out of there. That section also has an entrance from the meadow. I was never allowed to go to that area or the meadow for the entire time you were away. Do the tunnels go under that section of the Complex?" she inquired.

"Yes, there are tunnels there," Shar reported, "but they are not directly connected to the ones under the living quarters. You have to get to them through the alcove beside the Great Hall and that is a pretty busy place most of the time."

"There's got to be another entrance, somewhere," I retorted, "possibly from one of the suites in that section. Unfortunately, right now those suites are as tightly guarded as we are. I'm convinced we can get some answers to 'why' if we could just get to those rooms. There has to be someone who knows the tunnel designs in that section."

We decided it was time for us to separate. Each of us promised to find out as much as we could and arranged to meet back in my quarters later that night. As I watched them crawl into the vent, I had some misgivings about the entire enterprise. I also knew that a few qualms of apprehension would not stop my pursuit to find the answer to this intense security question.

When we reconvened later, each of us had our own valuable contributions to the overall picture. Shar had obtained some orbs of the maps drafted of the original Complex in that section. Myra had spent some time chatting with her 'companions' about why it was necessary for her to be accompanied everywhere she went. In her usual charming way...by whining...she learned they were very concerned about her safety. There were some important meetings occurring and some very powerful opponents to these meetings had made some rather nasty threats. They were only trying to keep her out of harms way: One, by ensuring she did not inadvertently pick up any information. Two, by physically keeping her out of sight of those who knew about her close association with Risan. Her well being could be used against Risan by the unscrupulous beings who opposed the success of the negotiations,

My contribution took a different direction. I was able to talk with one of my acquaintances who worked at the landing docks. By way of a craft person who served me my meal, I had indicated that since my return I had not been able to get in touch with some of my friends. She agreed to pass along an invitation to Salgo, letting him know I was back and resting in my quarters. He visited me a short time later. We chatted of many things, but most importantly he was very fatigued by the pressure of the heightened security. The ships that landed for the most part were either from Kala or another smaller star system on the far side of our galaxy called Starathea. Starathea had been struggling with Cyron, a larger neighboring system, trying to maintain their independence and avoid absorption. They had turned to the Kalens for assistance. The Kalen delegate had requested help from us because of our status as Universal Ambassadors. He wasn't sure how the talks were going but many causalities had arrived to be treated at our Healing Center. Constant surveillance had been set up to detect any Opposers. They were checking all arriving ships. They're also certain some had slipped into the Complex before it was sealed off. There is an all out alert. None have been found because the Opposers are very good at disguise and have blended into the population.

The "Oh No" Trio

That cemented it! We had to do something to help. After all, we were not babies to be kept safe in our mothers' arms. We devised a plan to help discover the Opposers (a name we gave them because we didn't know their true identity). The energy of most of the beings at the Complex is well known to us and possibly we could detect the impostors, even if they had shape-shifted into another form. The biggest obstacle was getting released from our confinement. Today's actions had not helped our cause. There had to be something we could do.

We decided to petition Ela and Sosja for help in lifting the restrictions, at least enough to allow us movement around the Complex. We could suggest some kind of homing device carried on our person. That might work. If we asked to share breakfast with them because we missed their company we could broach the subject then. United, in pleasant surroundings, with good refreshments, we might stand a better chance of convincing them. We drafted an invitation to be taken to their quarters.

I handed the message to the guard outside my door as Shar and Myra retreated through the tunnel vent.

Fifteen

After a wonderfully restful night's sleep, I awoke refreshed and rejuvenated. It was still a while before the morning meal would be ready so I decided to fill my time with some productive endeavor. I bathed and dressed in what I felt appropriate attire for the task ahead of me. I then gathered the map orbs and seated myself at my desk. These amazing little silver devices had the capacity to store volumes of information. Somewhere in them lie the exact data to facilitate our plan. I set about screening the contents. There was so much information I only hoped I could find what I needed quickly.

The maps were actually pictures of each location presented in sequence. We had long ago abandoned diagrams and drawings on physical material. They were bulky and subject to destruction. Aerial views using piercing rays gave detailed images of the matrix of tunnels running beneath the Complex. These were presented with subsequent shots of the interiors of each section. I could transfer these images into my large capacity memory bank to be retrieved, at will, later.

After much searching I finally located the quarters off the Great Hall. I identified the entrance at the alcove and noted the access code. I continued to search along the wing noting all entrances and exits from the tunnels. Most of these seemed to be accesses to the various suites. Toward the end of the wing farthest from the Great Hall there was a large meeting room with several entry points.

The "Oh No" Trio

Further down the wing there was an eating area where meals were served. Most of the food served throughout the Complex came from the main kitchen. What I really needed was an access point where we would not be noticed. All that I had encountered so far were much too exposed.

Eureka! Off the eating area there was a small kitchen to accommodate guests when the main kitchen was closed. This room was located at the very end of the wing right next to the doors leading out into the meadow. But most importantly it had an entry point to give us access without being seen. The entrance off the meadow must be the one Myra had mentioned. Perfect, we can make our way to that kitchen, under some pretense, and enter the maze of tunnels from there. We can then observe the happenings of every suite in the wing.

I was startled by a rap on my door. It was the guard letting me know breakfast was being served in the solarium. I hope we are successful in our attempt with Ela and Sosja. They agreed to the meal. Now let's hope our powers of persuasion are great enough to sway them to our cause. We can put Myra to work on them. She always has been able to accomplish the most amazing things with just a sweet smile and a battering of her eyelids.

It always amazed me how three such diverse beings could be as close as Shar, Myra, and I were. If age alone wasn't a factor, our differing personalities should have caused trouble. Maybe, it is the differences that make us click so well. We seem to complement each other's strengths. Shar has an ability to procure any item we have ever needed because of his wide circle of connections. He also has a talent for the technical that is just slightly different than mine. Where I can visualize the finished product, he seems to see all the parts needed to assemble it. We really work well as a team and always cover each other's back. Myra seems to fit in nicely and brings a bubbly, carefree feeling to every undertaking. *'Nothing is impossible'* for very long according to her. So we usually succeed in our adventures, even if they sometimes turn out very different than the original concept.

J.L. Alonzo

Leaving my quarters, I was accompanied down the hall to the solarium. The guard was pleasant, almost embarrassed at his assignment. He said he was a bit confused as to the need for such security. Yet, he knew the order had come from Risan and he wouldn't dream of countermanding it

Heavenly aromas drifted from the solarium through the open doors. The cooks must have really outdone themselves. I suddenly realized how very hungry I was. I had just picked at my dinner last night and my usual habit of a light snack before retiring had been pre-empted by the meeting with Shar and Myra.

The tables were set on the side of the solarium close to the windows. Ever aware of the effect of the surroundings on a being's state of mind, this room, like all others in the Complex, was in soft shades of sky and land. The sound of trickling water soothed the senses. A person was enticed to lounge in the soft pillow chairs nuzzled among an abundance of green growing foliage.

Ela and Sosja were standing by the serving table quietly speaking to the kitchen attendants who were arranging the selections they were taking off a large food cart. There was plenty of fresh fruit, a variety of cheeses, fresh baked breads, cold juices, and hot ciders. The absence of meat in the diet is an accepted fact in our kingdom. Most of the food we consume is grown and/or processed at one of the many outlining settlements. These are the same settlements where the medical herbs are produced. All living things are honored as having a special place in the Great Plan. Thanks are always given for what we consume to maintain life. All beings are provided for and here is no scarcity or lack, as likewise no greed of overindulgence. There just isn't a need.

Shar and Myra appeared at the door and proceeded into the room. My pondering had resulted in my being only a few steps from the doorway. They joined me and together we walked to the eating area. Silently, with a smile, Sosja handed each of us a plate and indicated that we should help ourselves to the food.

Once we were all seated, we gave thanks and everyone settled into enjoying the delicious entrees. Pleasant small talk passed between us as we progressed through the meal. Carefully we maneuvered the

The "Oh No" Trio

conversation toward the topic of our confinement. We proceeded to explain that all of the mishaps had been unintentional and we pleaded for tolerance. We further stated that we felt like prisoners. We knew it was not the practice of our culture to restrain other beings in an attempt to bend their will to ours. We explained that this is what we felt was happening to us. We employed them to assist us in securing our freedom.

Through the entire presentation Ela and Sosja placidly listened, very attentively, to our every word. But, visibly, they were unreadable. Had we made an impression? We were not sure.

Eventually the kitchen staff came to remove the food and clear the tables. As they restored the room to order, we moved to the more comfortable seating by the fountain. Once seated Ela began.

"My heart goes out to you for the predicament in which you find yourselves. Yet, I cannot see any way we might be of help to you. Believe me, Risan has not made his choices regarding you lightly. He truly understands you are free spirits. He also knows the results of your creativity. With situations as they are presently, he cannot afford the risk of another mishap. Maybe in a few more days, when the affects of this recent escapade have subsided I can talk to him and see if there might be some other arrangements we can make. But, for now, you must continue with the present restrictions. I'm truly sorry."

We knew this was the best we could hope for at this time. We also knew that we had penetrated Ela's shield and she would champion us to Risan when the timing was right. Ela and Sosja rose to leave. With sad faces, they opened their arms to us for hugs.

Well, that was that. We had given it our best shot. Now we must wait for an opportunity to present itself.

Sixteen

Opportunity sometimes knocks in the strangest way as we found out later that day. After breakfast with Ela and Sosja we settled into our studies. The topic was not one chosen by our instructors. We began, in earnest, plans to locate the Opposers who were somewhere in the Complex. We poured over all the information we had collected so far. I shared with Shar and Myra the images from the orbs through thought transfer. We outlined a route we could take within the wing of the Great Hall. We felt it best to have a pre-planned agenda so we could act quickly when we once again had freedom of movement.

Exhaustion over came us shortly after lunch and we decided to retire to our sleeping quarters for a nap. This had been an extremely fatiguing day on the mental level and our bodies were manifesting the need to recharge. Rest of the physical would, hopefully, mean rest for the mental.

As I floated into slumber I felt some disturbing vibrations hovering around my bed. I logged it to being over tired and willed myself to relax. Still, something continued to pester me, asking me to stay alert and prepared. Again I tried to shake off the feeling but it persisted with more strength. My help was needed.

Rolling off my bed and raising to my feet I thought, "O.K.! I'm up. Now what do I do?" I felt an invisible tug drawing me toward the tunnel entrance. Deep in the recesses of my mind I heard a

The "Oh No" Trio

whispered scream for help. I recognized the voice. It was Myra. She was in danger. I could feel it with every fiber of my being.

I dropped into the tunnel and hurried toward Shar's quarters. As I reached for the vent cover it was abruptly jerked up away from my grasp. Shar's eyes stared into mine.

"Did you hear it too?" he asked. "Can we follow her energy trail? She is so small and not really from this culture. We need to find her. She needs us."

As fast as the space permitted, we moved along the passage leading to Myra's sleeping quarters. Even from a distance we could see a shaft of light filtering into the tunnel directly below her vent.

Upon reaching the open vent we vaulted into her room hoping our worst fears would be unfounded. Instantly we knew that was not so. It was evident a struggle had taken place. An overturned table...a chair...several other items...were scattered around the room. The coverlet from her bed had been torn in half and only one part remained on the floor next to the vent. She hadn't gone easily and her energy vibrated with an intensity we had never felt. She was doing her best to leave a strong trail for us to follow. For she knew we would come and move heavens and earths to find her. Good girl!

We quickly re-entered the tunnel and sensed her energy leading down the cavern headed away from the living quarters. This part of the maze went under the kitchen area and out into the meadow. Briskly we covered the distance emerging into the fresh air. There was no one in sight anywhere on the meadow. Yet, her energy remained strong leading us around the outside of the Complex wall toward the opposite side by the Great Hall. They must be headed for the wing of suites where the visiting delegates were housed. This didn't make sense. That wing was under such heavy guard a mouse couldn't squeak by. Why there? You'd think the Opposers would want to get as far away from the Complex as possible. Unless, maybe their absence would be noticed and create more of a disturbance than their presence.

We rushed through the door and slipped into the small kitchen. So far so good. We easily located the entrance to the tunnel system.

J.L. Alonzo

Her energy was still very strong. We quickened our pace, our hope building. As we rounded a slight turn we came face to face with a stone wall. This could not be. It was not in the images we held in our minds.

Shar and I looked at each other with puzzled expressions. Instantly we shifted becoming thin streams of liquid. This shape allowed us to slip effortlessly beneath the wall.

Resuming our original form we continued down the tunnel, but slowly we came to a stop. We had lost her energy. That couldn't be. There were no vents in this area and definitely no turn-offs. We did a quick about face and retraced our steps. When we arrived at the spot where the wall should have been, we screeched to a stop. What? It should be right here! It was gone! But how?

Obviously the Opposers had more skills than we had given them credit for. It was clear now that they too could shape-shift. Probably, in our haste, we had missed detecting their energy. We had slipped beneath them as they stood there with Myra encased in their prison of stone.

We steadied ourselves and calmed our senses. Her energy had to be here somewhere. Faintly we began to pick up wisps of her energy. Her vibration was very weak. It led off to the right, down a smaller tunnel we had not noticed in our speedy passing.

We increased our pace again. Her energy became stronger. It led us deeper and deeper into the dimly lit cavern. More cautiously we proceeded, feeling our way along till our hands came to rest on a wall directly in our path. A dead end! Where? Where is she? Her energy was still very strong. In the dimness we looked around. A small sliver of light trickled through the ceiling above where we had just passed. We had missed it because we had been looking down.

On closer inspection we realized that the light was coming through a small grid that covered a vent. Now that we were standing still we could hear muffled voices but the language was unfamiliar to us.

Then, very distinctly we heard, "You're in big trouble! You can't do this to me! They'll find me and you'll be punished!" Myra was

The "Oh No" Trio

putting up her heroic brave front. If only she knew how true her words were.

Only at that moment did we realize how ill-prepared we were for a rescue attempt. We had not even left a message so help could follow. We only had ourselves. Silently I reached for the grid. Gently, I slid it to the side. I sure hoped her captors were looking the other way. I shifted into the shape of a snake and slithered up into the room. I could see Myra seated in a chair by the far wall. Two beings stood in front of her. I did not recognize their origins.

Shar, following my lead slithered to my side. We exchanged knowing looks and proceeded across the room. As we closed the distance between us and the captors we picked up speed. Just as we reached them, we snapped our bodies to coil. Wrapped around the legs of one of the beings I heard him bellow as he descended toward the floor. Out of the corner of my eye I saw that Shar had followed suit. Just before our victims hit the floor we wrenched ourselves free and recoiled around their chests. Tighter and tighter I constricted cutting off my victim's air. He clutched at me but was not able to break my hold on him. Slowly, he slumped unconscious to the floor. I looked toward Shar and saw that he had successfully disabled his prey.

Satisfied that the two were completely incapacitated we reshaped into out true form and collected Myra. We lead her quickly to the tunnel vent. Shar descended first. I handed Myra down to him and then swiftly followed. I replaced the grid and started after Shar and Myra who were already moving rapidly down the passageway. From above I heard muffled sounds. Myra's captors were regaining consciousness.

Running as fast as we could we covered the distance between the suite and the small kitchen. We all but ejected ourselves through the vent to be greeted by a pair of strong hands and the smiling face of Risan.

Seventeen

Down the hall from the kitchen we heard the shuffling of feet and realized the guards had reached the room where Myra had been held captive. As we stepped from the kitchen we saw the two beings escorted from the suite and down the hallway toward the Great Hall. Puzzled, I glanced around me. Sosja stepped forward to enfold me in her arms. Ela held Myra and Risan stood beside Shar with his arm wrapped around Shar's shoulder.

"How did you know?" I sputtered. "How did you get here so fast?"

"We had you monitored," Shanar replied, as he stepped from the shadows behind me. "We had been suspicious of the activity of some of the delegates and figured if we fed you enough enticing information you would feel compelled to investigate. The one thing we never counted on was Myra's capture. But, that was the result of her extreme curiosity. She hoped to solve the mystery by herself and surprise you with the news. But, it seems she was the one surprised."

"All is well now," Risan inserted. "Come, let's all return to our living quarters and we will share everything with you."

"Do you mind if we walk back outside the building, in the meadows?" I asked. "I definitely feel the need for some wonderfully fresh air."

The "Oh No" Trio

Strolling leisurely through the sweet smelling grass, feeling the warmth on my back with a light breeze kissing my face, brought me into balance again. I knew that indeed things had been set right. There had been much more to the 'why' than we thought. To think we had been used as pawns. To think Risan and Shanar felt us capable of such a task. That was the truly amazing part. It certainly changed the picture in my mind. We weren't just three screw-ups, but a useful team who could produce successful results. I smiled, my heart lightened. What a day!

When we arrived at the living quarters the entire scene had changed. Many people were gathered in the hallway to greet us and express their delight with our actions. They inquired about our well being and congratulated us on our success. As we entered the solarium many stood and applauded. Tables were set all around the fountain with many lavish dishes.

Risan led our party to the main table and once everyone was seated, musicians entered and began to entertain us with a new ballad titled *The Tenacious Trio*. It was all a little overwhelming. I turned to my mother seated next to me, raising my eyebrow in question. She simply smiled, then leaned over to place a kiss on my cheek. In a hushed voice she said, "I'm so proud of you. It has been very hard maintaining my distance so the plan could play out. You have definitely confirmed our trust in your instincts and skills."

As everyone began to partake of the food, a gentle murmur of conversation floated through the room. The evening was undeniably one of the best in my life. As the time passed, many of the visiting delegates joined us and chatted. They expressed their thanks and relief at having the menace of the Opposers lifted from the meetings. The very next day, a formal signing of the alliance would take place at an outside ceremony. This news made it a truly festive affair. The merriment lasted for many hours.

Even the Kalan Ambassador appeared, briefly, to congratulate us on a job well done. This was a great concession on his part, considering our ages. His remarks caused smile to creep across Risan's face as he looked my way. It seems we may have redeemed ourselves, at least a little, in the eyes of this formidable dignitary.

J.L. Alonzo

In private, low voices Shanar and Risan explained how they had been able to trace our every movement by the use of a fragrance they had applied to our clothing and skin. They did confess there had been some tense moments when it became evident that Myra had been captured. Yet. they had forced themselves to remain quiet so as not to alert the Opposers. Even now they are not sure they apprehended all members of the coup. Many extra precautions are still in place to guarantee the safety of the guests and participants of tomorrow's ceremony.

I was exhausted beyond belief, as I excused myself and retired to my room. My mind buzzed with all the details Uncle Risan had shared concerning all the happenings that had led up to the alliance. It had been a long, arduous endeavor with many key players. I felt honored to be part of such an illustrious group.

In a haze of love and serenity I plopped onto my bed and floated into the sleep state, yet held on to just a touch of excited anticipation for what tomorrow would hold.

Eighteen

The mood in the air was one of great optimism. There were people bustling about in all areas of the Complex. It felt like heaven to be free to travel wherever I chose. The restrictions...every one of them...had been lifted. Dressed in my most festive and regal attire, I strolled briskly across the plaza in front of the Great Hall. Banners hung from every wall on the buildings that flanked the magnificent tile-floored area. Seating had been erected to accommodate those anxious to attend this momentous occasion. The signing would cement relations between Starathea and the Star System Council. This alliance would guarantee Starathea's security as an independent kingdom by providing aide and support from the many star systems that are members of the council. This is indeed good.

Securely I tucked a small box under my arm and proceeded past the Great Hall toward the meadow. After the official signing at a ceremony held in the plaza, there was to be a banquet served in the glorious outdoors in the meadow.

I just hoped I could find some free time. I really wanted to experiment with a new toy given to me by Shar. He found it on his trip with Konal and brought it to me in my quarters just this morning. Because of all the excitement since his return he had totally forgotten about it. It was a small space craft fashioned after our own larger ones. Except, this one could be remotely controlled by thought impulses. My plan is to take it up onto the hill beside the Complex so I can practice with it. I'd like to get familiar with the operation commands. This is just the day for such a pleasant adventure.

Shar and Myra were already waiting for me in the center of the meadow. We proceeded away from the Complex and started up the hill. The last time we visited this place was the day of that terrible accident with the band platform. I sincerely hoped we didn't have a repeat of that experience. Of course, how could we? The platform was already in place and properly secured. Even so, we decided to bypass the tower and practice our flight maneuvers up by the large tree that stood on the crest of the hill.

Many times that lovely old tree had allowed us to climb into it's highest branches. What a magnificent view from that lofty perch. One could see all of the meadow, the splendor of the Complex beside it, and beyond to the sparkling sea. It was truly breathtaking. A light breeze flowed through the grass and rustled the leaves of the great tree. We settled ourselves at the tree's base facing the sea. For a while, we just sat there taking in every sensation. It was so nourishing. I felt more alive than I had for quite some time.

I placed the box on the ground between Shar and myself. My mind wandered, reviewing all that had happened over these past days. I thought of the danger and excitement. I tingled at the memories of the party and the joy and happiness it brought. I expanded, remembering the look of pride in my mother's eyes and likewise, in the eyes of Ela. Mostly, I felt elated that I was again within the good graces of Uncle Risan. I thought of the ceremony and the signing that would take place. We would then enjoy a fantastic banquet. The warmth and serenity must have been like a tranquilizer to us for all three of us drifted off into a soft but deep sleep.

I'm not sure how long we slept but when I awoke I could hear voices down in the meadow. I nudged Shar and Myra to wake them. If we were going to enjoy this toy we had better get cracking, for soon there would be too much happening. We were expected to attend the ceremony and banquet.

I opened the lid of the box and removed the small craft. It was fabulous; an exact replica of the small crafts we use for intra-stellar travel. The directions for operation seemed clear enough: Think it and it is so. Yet, I imagine that could get a little tricky, depending on a person's thoughts.

I looked at Shar and he smiled. I switched on the toy. It began to hum...a low deep melodious hum. The bridge began to pulse with brilliant blue, green, yellow, and red lights. These lights vibrated to the beat of the hum. As I held it in my hands I began to think wonderful thoughts of a smooth flight, gentle turns and an easy landing in the lush grass. I could feel the craft pulling to be free to follow my thoughts, so I released it.

It was a truly beautiful sight shimmering in the light and moving gracefully through the air. I thought of a long gentle loop and it responded. Then I thought of it flying sideways, circling the massive base of the tree and again it complied. It was doing precisely what my mind was thinking. This was magnificent. I thought of it flying over to Myra and landing softly in her lap and it performed perfectly. Next, I thought of it buzzing around Shar's head and landing 'kerplop' right on top. Again it responded, causing all three of us to laugh with delight. How wonderful! I continued to maneuver it thus for quite some time. Myra begged for a turn and I surrendered the craft to her. She had it doing loop-de-loops and climbing straight up, then turning to come, at a very high rate of speed, down to the ground only to land gently on the grass. Shar took a turn. He really put it through the paces: High speeds close to the ground. Intricate paths through the branches of the tree. It seemed to just barely miss, yet never touched, the tender leaves.

As I retrieved control of the craft, again, I heard voices in the meadow. I wondered what time it was getting to be. The craft responded to my thoughts by heading out, full speed, in the direction of the tower clock at the complex. This would never do. I thought it back, but the distance between myself and the ship must have been too great for my thought waves to reach it clearly. The craft sputtered and jostled through the air, trying to return to the crest of the hill.

I looked down into the meadow. The many banquet tables were laden with food and the guests were already seated. At Risan's head table, the guests were beginning their meal. The soup had been served. Risan and the Kalan Ambassador were engaged in conversation as the ate. Oh no, I thought. What if the craft malfunctioned and landed in Risan's bowl.

Instantly I realized my error. The craft was again within range to pick up my thoughts. The directions for operating this toy were crystal clear: *Think it and so it is!*

Splash! As the craft landed in its assigned location, soup flew from the dish. Large amounts of liquid splattered into Risan's face and onto his clothes. Because the Kalan Ambassador had been leaning close to say something right at that moment, he too was delivered with a goodly portion of the displaced liquid. Abruptly, Risan rose bellowing for a server to come with towels. As he waited he scanned the horizon. He spotted us just as he applied the towel to the liquid dripping from his chin.. His eyes met mine. Without words, I nodded for I knew exactly the message he was sending.

Does there always have to be a mishap? I looked at Shar and Myra. Their shocked looks must have mirrored mine. We grasped each others' hand and began to descend the hill. We headed for the living quarters and another meeting with Risan.

Nineteen

To face Risan again was more than we could stand. We talked of many options as we walked toward the Complex. We did have alternatives. Maybe we should exercise one of them. We agreed on a plan. We would leave the Complex and go out to live on our own, away from any proximity to the official happenings in Risan's household. That would solve many of the problems everyone was experiencing.

We didn't even need to collect anything from the living quarters. We could manifest what we needed when we found the right place for us. So we turned off and took the trail that led into the hills. There were many places we could go. We would find a lovely valley with pools and streams. We would find our place on this star and the universe would provide.

The burden of guilt began to lift and it became lighter the farther we traveled away from the Complex. Soon there was a spring to our steps and smiles on our faces. This was the perfect solution and it also promised to hold great adventure.

Fatigue finally compelled us to stop and rest. We had covered quite a distance. The scenery around us was very picturesque. We had entered this enchanting valley some time back and had been so intent on moving on we had been oblivious to our pristine surroundings. The peacefulness was almost physical. There seemed to be magic all around us. (Every fiber of my body tingled with

J.L. Alonzo

anticipation.) As we looked at each other we knew...this was where we belonged.

We began in earnest to select a suitable site to manifest our lodgings. A pond of emerald blue water was located below a cascade of gently falling water just off the center of the valley. There were lush groves of green trees and shrubs flanking the valley on each side climbing up the hills. Wildflowers dotted the landscape. A small stream meandered away from the pond toward the sea in the far distance. No more beautiful spot could be imagined anywhere in this galaxy...or for that matter, the entire universe.

Already it felt like home. We could feel it reaching out to embrace us in its love and protection. We decided on individual quarters of oval construction set in a semicircle. We brought into being a larger structure that would provide us with an eating area, a workshop, and a small chapel. We exercised our skill of manifesting by bringing into our site the items needed to sustain our lives and provide comfort.

The days flew by as we continued to envision, then manifest, our settlement. It took on a personality that was a complementary blending of the three distinct yet harmonious beings who were creating it.

Finally, it was complete. As we stood and admired our handiwork we were indeed pleased with what we saw. We decided that a celebration was in order and we dressed splendidly for the occasion. We fixed dishes that were sure to satisfy any appetite. Shar played his flute and Myra and I danced to the lilting melody. Life could not have been more perfect.

As life settled into some kind of routine we kept ourselves busy with the things we loved most. Shar even taught Myra to play the flute and she became very good. I pursued my investigation into natural healing properties of the plants found in the valley. This was a curiosity that had come to the front while I was in Uncle Shanar's class in the field. We even manifested a small laboratory for chemical analysis.

As naive as we were, we thought we could go on forever this way. It never occurred to us that our absence would cause concern or alarm for those who cared for us.. Or, that we should be cautious, till one day when I was out gathering specimens I could feel a presence but didn't see anyone. When I returned to the settlement I shared my experience with Shar and Myra. They too had experienced similar happenings. We decided to try and be more aware. We even considered returning to the Complex to let our family know where we were.

Over the next couple of days we were more and more aware of the presence. It seemed very familiar, but I couldn't place why. The energy had a distinct vibration, but a definite identification just wasn't there. It would come to us, we felt. We just had to try harder to remember.

After much discussion we decided to relax and settle into our normal activities. Amazingly, that decision caused the energy to subside and eventually we couldn't feel it at all. Maybe it was from another area and had finally returned to its domain. But, why had it traveled here in the first place? Had it followed us here? Was it as curious about us as we were about it? We would probably never know.

One day, as I was working in the laboratory, Shar approached saying he had a restless feeling and was going to do some exploring. I nodded without even looking up. So totally absorbed in my work I didn't even note the time he left. I didn't even see which direction he went. The day flew by and fatigue set in. I decided to stretch my tired and strained muscles. I rose and exited the lab, then stopped abruptly. *Something was not right!* The settlement was in complete disarray. Items were scattered everywhere. Myra was nowhere to be seen and neither was Shar. I called and to my right heard a meek voice cry out, "Over here!" Myra was crouched behind one of the trees on the far side of the pond. Rushing to her I asked, "What happened?"

"I don't know exactly," she replied. "I was gathering wildflowers when a strong wind blew into the settlement. It tossed items about and overturned everything in it's path. Then it headed up the path in the direction Shar took. I was so frightened I was unable to move. I feared for you working in the lab. I had the strangest feeling I was

J.L. Alonzo

watching something alive. It was like it had a plan and was looking for something or someone specific. What do you think it was?"

"I couldn't even guess," I said. "What direction did it go?"

Myra motioned toward the mountains without saying a word. I asked, "Where is Shar?"

She looked at me bewildered. "He left this morning to go exploring. I'm really worried because I thought he'd be back by now."

I remembered then Shar's appearance at the lab. Why hadn't I been more alert and gotten some details about where he was going.

"Do you think he's all right?" she asked.

"I don't know," I replied, "but let's go see if we can find him. He may need our help."

"But, **that** is the same way that thing went!" said Myra. "How can we be sure it won't turn on us."

"We don't, but we have to chance it for Shar's sake," I replied. And with that we set off down the path in hopes of finding our friend.

Twenty

Shar's energy was easy to follow. He and I were so connected that I could detect even mere wisps of his essence in large crowded places. Here in the open air he left an even stronger trail. The residue energy from the entity that had swept through the settlement was also very strong and it seemed to be following Shar.

I wonder what he went 'exploring' for...bits of his conversation were flashing back into my mind. I wish I had paid closer attention but I was so absorbed in my experiment I wasn't aware of much of anything. He had mentioned something about an additional energy source and mobility. But, how could he hope to find such things out here in the wilderness. Of course, Shar had a brilliant scientific mind and was very good at developing alternate solutions for very complex problems.

As we hurried through the countryside my anxiety grew. For some reason I was very tense and nervous...on alert, as if danger were very near. Almost like a bolt of lightning it struck me. The energy from the entity was the same as the energy I felt in the tunnels when we were searching for Myra! Yet then I was so concentrated on Myra's energy I had barely registered the other energies I was picking up.

I thought that matter had been handled. The culprits had been apprehended. Maybe there were more. The alliance had been formed...signed, sealed, and delivered...but that certainly didn't mean the Opposers would stop there. But why is this entity following Shar? What is it looking for that it didn't find at the settlement? It had virtually torn the place apart.

I suddenly felt a real urgency to get to Shar so I increased my pace. Myra was literally running to keep up with me. I glanced back and the fear in her eyes reached out to touch me.

"I feel it too," she said breathlessly. "It's the same energy I felt when I was captured. Will they now get Shar? Will they hurt him? What can we do?"

I quickly turned and gathered her into my arms, giving her a warm reassuring hug. "He has defenses he can use and I'm sure he will," I whispered against her head. I released her as quickly as I had collected her, turned and hurried on. We must find Shar...soon. (We are always stronger in the company of those we love and trust. We need to add our energy to his.) I immediately began sending out my light and love to him. I tried to connect my mind to his so we could communicate. I called but got no answer. Determined, I called again and this time received a very faint reply. I upped my vibration and called a third time.

"Shar, what is your location and condition?" I thought with great intensity.

"I'm hiding in a maintenance building next to the airstrip at the Space Training Facility. There seems to be an energy storm blowing outside. It came upon me while I was on the trail so I ducked in here," came his response.

I quickly reported what had happened at the settlement. I never broke stride, hoping to cover as much distance as possible. We had quite a hike ahead of us for we were several kilometers away and traveling switchback mountain trails.

Suddenly I was struck with an idea. What if I teleported to his location? I had just begun training on this skill and I wasn't sure I could be successful. Besides, I didn't know if Myra was capable of doing teleporting. She was from a far different system than this one and not all beings have developed this gift. I stopped for a moment to ask her. She said it was not something she could do because of some unique circumstances that were too complicated to

The "Oh No" Trio

discuss right then. I made a decision. I would send her back to the Complex for help and teleport myself to Shar so I could help him in the meantime. I was sure the energy storm he was experiencing had something to do with the entity that had visited us earlier at the settlement.

I related my plan to Myra. As she set off to retrace our path to the fork that turned off to the Complex I began to collect myself. I tried to remember what was required to exercise this gift. The object was to picture where it is you want to go and see yourself there. It helped to visualize the person you were seeking and their energy would be a beacon, lighting the way for your molecules.

I pictured Shar as I remembered him this morning as he stood in the lab. I then relaxed into the tingling energy I felt begin to envelop my body. There was absolutely nothing but light all around me. I had no sensation of color, temperature, or movement. I was just part of that brilliant light. I had no feeling of time or distance. I just was. Then, the light began to change, taking on different colors that floated around me as a mist. There were no definite forms. Gradually shapes began to form. My sense of touch began to return and I reached for one of the shapes that looked like a hand. Indeed it was a hand. It was Shar's hand. It was holding mine and his eyes were staring at me in astonishment.

"What have you done?" he asked, his voice echoing in my head. " How did you get here? One minute I was alone and the next you were by my side."

I tried to speak but no sound came from my mouth. My body had not completely resolidified. I waited. I watched the changing expressions on Shar's face. It seemed like an eternity. Finally, I uttered, in the barest of whisper..."I teleported!"

Twenty-One

Shar grabbed me, holding me tight, and I felt the solidness of his form. I began to giggle...and the giggle turned into a chuckle...then the chuckle turned into laughter...and the laughter developed into rolling laughter and howls of delight coming from the two of us as we shook each other in disbelief. What a glorious way to travel.

The light that had surrounded me was gone and I realized we were encased in darkness. There were very few windows in the maintenance shed. I allowed myself to adjust to my surroundings. "Have you a plan?" I asked.

"Yes," replied Shar, "but it will have to be modified to accommodate two. I thought I would be in this alone. The training crafts are located just outside this building a short distance away. I figured on borrowing one and surveying the area to try and discover what I could about the disturbance. The storm didn't appear to be a natural occurrence. I thought an aerial view would give more information. I was almost here when it overtook me. Do you remember how to fly a training craft?"

Smiling I nodded. Shar placed his hand on the door latch and slowly slid it to the side. Uncertain what we might find, we cautiously eased ourselves outside. We stood back to back so we could protect each other.

All was calm again outside and a few meters away one of the small intra-stellar crafts sat silently on it's launching platform. Swiftly we raced across the terrain and entered the craft. As the hatch closed behind us we breathed a sigh of relief. So far, so good!

Our training on these crafts had been rather sketchy to date. Everyone in the kingdom is required to have a working knowledge of them. Most of the instruction had been general...just what was needed in case of an emergency. This precaution had proved wise on several occasions when crafts were in trouble and the pilot was incapable of operating it. Still, we were more than a little nervous about borrowing it. Yet, this indeed was a dire situation for we needed to collect Myra and return to the Complex as quickly as possible. Plus, the aerial observations we would make could be very helpful in dealing with the menace.

Shar fitted himself into the control seat while I took the attendant's position. Shar had more experience operating these vehicles because of his expeditions with Konal. At the touch of his hand the craft sprang to life. The gentle hum of the Photon powered generators made me feel much more at ease. I concentrated on the panel in front of me. I began to key in the coordinates for our settlement. I fed in the variables needed to accommodate the switchback mountain trail. We couldn't be sure where we would find Myra. I added the specs for the proposed flight from the fork to the Complex. Hopefully we could intercept Myra before she traveled very far. I had lost track of how long it had been since I left her. That teleporting business made it hard for me to accurately determine how much time had passed.

Having fed all the necessary data into the computer, I hit the engage button. The craft sprang from the platform, straight up, and we were airborne. When I turned to smile at Shar I noticed the scowl on his face. "What?" I asked.

"Something is creating a drag on the ship," he said. "Did you feel the engines gear down? I don't see anything but there sure is a lot of dust blowing around. That isn't common for a craft this size."

"Could we have been discovered by the tower?" I inquired. "Maybe they have trained a resistor beam on us."

"I'm not picking up any readings," he replied. "Those beams usually peg the meters when they're used. I've advanced the torque but we still aren't moving. Engage an anti-interference shield and see if that breaks us free."

I turned to the panel in front of me and requested the activation of the shield. The computer responded, "Unable to engage shielding." At the same moment Shar employed the power booster and like a pebble in a slingshot the craft broke free and propelled skyward. Talk about whiplash! I felt like my head was going to snap off my body.

Shar eased back on the power and we leveled off but the thrust had lifted us too high to make visual surveillance of the Facility. I switched on the heat seeking probes and the screen in front of me sprang to life. Most of the window was a cool blue...the reflected color of natural terrain. I requested the computer to scan the Space Training Facility. A superimposed template of the Facility identified the building and roadways. As the screen moved a large red oval appeared. Red was the indicator of a high vibrational energy presence. The oval was moving...straight toward the tower. Shar banked the ship and came into line behind the oval. We followed the path it had taken. Shar accelerated to close the distance. He added altitude with a hope of coming above the oval and getting a look down inside. As we entered it's perimeter we realized there was no ceiling to this energy field. We could not climb above it. I felt the engines reverse and looked quickly at Shar. He pointed to the magnetic field indicator. It was almost pegged. That thing had to be dragging us in. Shar again hit the power booster and within a few seconds...which seemed like years...we broke free. We surmised that the energy wasn't strong around the edges. We decided to circle it and see if we could take some readings. If we could determine it's circumference we could use that information to pinpoint it's center. We could feed the data into the computer and it would relate it to the oval on the screen.

We also realized there was a more pressing problem. The storm field was quickly closing the distance between itself and the tower. We opened communication in an attempt to warn the tower crew. We couldn't communicate! The energy field must be neutralizing the signal. We had to warn the tower even though we weren't certain of

The "Oh No" Trio

the capabilities or intent of the storm field. I decided to try sending a mental message. I had been to the tower many times during my visits to the Facility. I trained my thought toward the small control room on the top floor. That was the most likely place the crew would be at this time. I focused and projected my thoughts.

"This is Sealo. Close the shields and prepare for an emergency. Force field heading your way and am not certain of it's intent or capabilities."

I repeated the thought message over and over, increasing the intensity with each transmission. My eyes were glued to the tower, which was now visible in front of us. As the metal shields slid into place, covering the viewing panels, I released the breath I hadn't realized I was holding. They heard me. Hopefully they are safe for the time being. Now on to other fish that require our attention.

"Shar, we had better head for the Complex and alert Risan. We don't have a prayer of being effective against that thing in this craft," I said. I turned back to the panel in front of me and activated the flight plan I had set. The craft banked and headed toward the mountains.

As we glanced back toward the tower we could see dust rising all around it. We knew the energy storm had reached it. We could only hope everything was all right for the crew.

Twenty-Two

We intercepted Myra a few kilometers from the Complex. As the craft settled down on its landing prongs, she ran toward us. Her clothes were covered with dust and her breath was coming in gasps. She must have run the entire distance. Beads of moisture had mixed with the dirt on her face and streams of muddy water were running from her forehead down to her chin.

She grabbed my extended hand and I helped her to one of the couches in the passenger area of the ship. As she plopped down, she tried to speak but she was still out of breath. I turned and closed the hatch. As Shar set the craft in motion, I placed my hands on a nearby table to maintain my balance. I worked my way over to the couch and helped Myra lie down.

"Just rest," I said, as I positioned a pillow under her head. I was surprised she had made it as far as she had. She must have really put on the speed. She turned on her side and closed her eyes. I dimmed the lighting over the couch area and returned to my seat. She would sleep for a while. I knew she really deserved it after what she'd been through.

As we neared the Complex we could see that many people were gathered in the plaza outside the Great Hall. Shar set the craft down easily and we swung the bay door open and lowered the stairs. As Shar disembarked, I went to check on Myra. She was still sleeping so I decided not to disturb her. She'd had a pretty rough day.

As I left the craft I scanned the crowd. I spotted Shar standing with Risan and Shanar. By the speed of Shar's mouth movement and hand action I guessed that he was relating our experiences. I eased myself up to the trio and listened as Shar shared his information.

Risan turned toward me. "We received a message from the tower at the Space Training Facility. They said you had been there and they thanked you for the warning. There wasn't any damage. The storm field just passed by them. Then, a short distance from the Facility, it vanished into the sky. It just lifted and was gone."

"They did pick up some unusual readings," he continued. "Some of the properties are not found on this star...for that matter...not even in this star system. We are running an analysis on the components. We're trying to determine their capabilities. You were wise to return to the Complex. We feel this may have something to do with the incident in the tunnel. The Complex is on alert. We hope to get to the heart of this soon."

The fatigue was beginning to take hold. I felt as if I was floating, and from time to time my vision blurred. Sounds crackled in my ears. I envied Myra asleep in the craft. As I glanced toward the craft, Shanar's words came clear:

"The alliance has many Opposers. We can't be sure we are dealing with the same ones. Besides, you said they seemed to be searching for something."

Refocusing my attention I said, "Yes, at the settlement the energy field just swept through. Then it followed Shar's trail across the mountains to the Training Facility. Shar is there any reason you should be the focus of such a undaunted pursuit?"

"Not that I'm aware of," he replied. "Except maybe when I was out with Konal on the latest expedition. I may have acquired something I may be shouldn't have. But I really can't think what. Besides, all those treasures remained here at the Complex when we left."

"Maybe we should visit your quarters and see what we can discover," Shanar injected. "If we have something they feel is important to them and return it, they may leave. Then, we can stand down the Complex."

J.L. Alonzo

Our small group maneuvered through the milling crowd and entered the living quarters. I made myself be aware of the energy around us. Barely noticeable, yet it was here. That same energy I felt when following Myra in the tunnel and Shar in the mountains. It should have dissipated by now because of the length of time that has passed. But, it was still here. The closer we came to Shar's quarters the stronger it got.

Risan opened the door and a blast of it hit me so strongly I stumbled slightly, bumping Shar. I could see by his eyes he too was aware. As I stepped further into the quarters I felt the energies begin to settle and become distinct. Off to the left of the door was a large display case that hung on the wall. The use of glass and lighting made it very visible and on the shelves were gems Shar had collected in his travels. The energy was definitely coming from that case. I moved toward it. Shar was at my side.

Shar hastened his pace reaching the case before the rest of us. He lifted a magnificent crystal from its resting place and held it up for us to see. It was breathtaking. It measured about fifteen centimeters across and twenty centimeters high. Its color was like nothing I'd ever seen before. This crystal was definitely the source of the energy I was picking up. "We were exploring a small star in a remote quadrant of our system when I found this," Shar related. "There were crystals everywhere. There appeared to be no beings inhabiting the star. This stone caught my attention, as if it were calling me. All I could see was it's beauty. I felt I had to have it to grace my gem case. I was simply overwhelmed by it's essence. I neglected to do the customary courtesy of checking to see if any elementals dwelled in it. I didn't even ask it if it wanted to leave with me. I've shown it to no one. I didn't even think to show it to Konal when I returned to the ship."

"Well, maybe it's time we made it's acquaintance," said Risan. "Look deeply into it and ask if a being lives within. If one answers ask it to come forth and speak to us so we can ask it's forgiveness."

As if by magic the crystal began to pulse and glow. A fragile feminine voice spoke, "Why have you captured me and taken me from my home?"

"I did not know you were there," whispered Shar, his voice cracking with remorse. "In my excitement at finding you I neglected to inquire. We thought your star was uninhabited. We had not detected any life form."

"*We* are a life. My people inhabit that star. Every crystal there is an individual being. When visitors arrive we have the capabilities of going dormant so we are undetected. But, I must admit when you arrived I was very curious about you. I decided to open a little so I could learn more. Dormant we are quite dull but open we have a brilliance."

"Yes, that is what attracted me to you," Shar replied. "I was dazzled by the iridescent luster of your light. I had never encountered such beauty. I am very sorry for the trauma I have put you through. What can I do to return you to your people? They have been searching for you and when last seen they vanished into the sky above the mountains."

"If they are here on your star I can contact them," she said excitedly. With that the Crystal began to glow and pulse more dynamically, sending out a rainbow of rays. There was a definite rhythm to the pulsing. Presently, the pulse and glow diminished and her small voice again reached our ears.

"They will wait for me. They were preparing to depart your star because they had not found any trace of my energy, only Shar's. His energy had been picked up by my people around the spot where he found me. It was the only clue they had. Can you take me to them, Shar?" she asked.

Shar turned to Risan, who gave him a nod. "Yes," he replied. "I would be honored."

Twenty-Three

We entered the craft, Shar carrying the Crystal and me loaded with a 'little snack' that Sosja and Ela had prepared for us. We had enough food to feed an army of hungry Cycrons, but mothers are notorious for making sure their offspring are fed to the max.

Myra was just waking up from her nap. She stretched and, as her eyes focused on the food, she sprang from the couch and scurried to the table. "I'm starved," she retorted, as she grabbed a piece of ripe fruit. "Did anything important happen while I was asleep?"

Shar and I burst into fits of laughter. "You might think so after we fill you in," Shar replied. He carefully placed the Crystal, wrapped in a velvet cloth, on a leisure chair next to the couch Myra had been sleeping on. He then returned to the operations area and seated himself at the control panel. "But, that information will have to be given in transit. Our immediate concern is getting this craft airborne and returning a priceless treasure to some very anxious beings."

A look of startled surprise lit up Myra's face as she rushed over to where our passenger sat. Slowly, she unwrapped the cloth and gasped, open mouth, at the exposed Crystal. Crystal began to pulse sending off an angelic hum and magnificent pink and gold rays. "Who is this delightful creature?" asked the petite feminine voice of the Crystal.

The "Oh No" Trio

Myra leapt back in astonishment. "How marvelous!" she squealed. "Where ever did you find her?"

Shar touched the ignition and the engines leapt to life. In a lightly sarcastic tone of voice, he replied, "Oh, its just a little something I picked up in my travels, quite to my...and likewise your...misfortune."

As the craft smoothly climbed and departed from the Complex we began to relate the story.

We were nearing the mountains by the time we had brought Myra up to date. Her constant interruptions...questions and exclamation... had prolonged the explanation. Shar reduced the engine power and we started a leisurely descent toward our rendezvous point.

"How could you have been so insensitive?" Myra asked. "We all know full well there are many sophisticated and highly intelligent civilizations in the universe. These species may take any form. Usually you are more aware and can pick up on the energy of a life form before the technical equipment can. I just don't understand"

"As I said," remarked Shar, "we had determined there weren't any signs of life on the star. Besides, the Crystals are able to become dormant to disguise themselves."

As the craft settled down onto the ground the sound of dust particles hitting the outer shell terminated the conversation.

"They are here," the Crystal being reported. "It will be good to see those of my own kind. I will be glad to return home to my star. It has been very lonely and frightening here."

" They must really be excited, judging by the storm outside. Is there any way your can get them to tone it down so we can open the hatch?" I asked.

The Crystal began to glow and brilliant rainbow rays shot from her in every direction. The color filled the cabin. The rays, also, seemed to be penetrating the hull of the ship for we could see the same colors outside through the viewing panel. We then realized the colors were traveling in spirals and not straight lines. They were like her rays but they were coming from a different source. Actually, they were coming from many other sources. Slowly the storm calmed and the dust subsided. I reached for the handle, turned it and slid the hatch aside. The ground around the craft was covered with Crystals. As the steps lowered to the surface the Crystals moved to allow the footing to settle.

Shar stood and walked toward our passenger. "I am really terribly sorry for my actions," he said as he lifted the Crystal. "I promise to be more vigilant in the future. This whole situation has taught me a very valuable lesson."

"I can tell by your energy you have a very beautiful heart," the Crystal being said. "I feel no trace of malice there."

The four of us proceeded from the craft and were met by the most glorious humming. It was like a host of angelic voices reaching into our heart and soul. The love in the tone was breath-taking. Slowly we were able to pick up the words of the song. "Hail beloved Princess! We surround you with our love." Over and over these phrases were repeated.

"Princess?" blurted Shar. "But...but..."

His stammering was preempted by movement among the Crystals. A group of five emissaries stepped forward. One, very large, Crystal spoke. "Beloved Princess, we have found you at last. We rejoice in your recovery. We hope you have fared well. We were so distraught at your disappearance. We did not think we could be successful. There were not many clues to follow. We only had the energy beam of this creature here." At that he pointed to Shar. "We had searched this entire star and were about to give up hope."

"I'm so very glad your didn't," replied the Princess. "I so want to return to my home. Yet, I must inform you that in your search you have created quite a disturbance for the inhabitants of this star. I fear you owe them an apology."

Shar stepped forward saying, "No, as I said before, it is I who apologize and beg your forgiveness. I am even more disconcerted by your title."

"Did I neglect to mention that to you?" replied the Crystal Lady. "Titles are of small consequence to me. To me all life forms are priceless royalty...since we are all part of the One. I often forget that on some worlds being a Princess is a most sought after and prestigious position. Having been one my entire life I place no great value on it." She then sighed and again sent out her colorful aura.

The large Crystal emissary began to pulse and in a booming male voice retorted, "It is time we departed. They, at home, await us. We have sent forth the news of your recovery and our people are anxious to welcome you home."

"But, where is your craft?" I asked, looking around and seeing none.

"We have cloaked it. It is not necessary to uncloak for us to board. We prefer our technology remain undiscovered, as we ourselves wish to remain so. We prefer our privacy," he replied.

Shar placed the Crystal Princess on the ground near the delegates and stepped back. The group moved toward an open area off to our right. The rest of the Crystals followed. One by one they vanished... as if into thin air. Soon just the three of us stood there alone. We heard a gentle purring of an engine but gradually that too faded away.

"That is it, I guess," remarked Shar. "I didn't even really say good-bye."

"There is no need for good-byes," spoke the lovely voice of the Crystal Princess through the still air. "I extend to you an invitation to visit us whenever you like. We will always welcome you as a new and valued friend."

The air returned to its stillness and we knew they were gone.

Twenty-Four

"Whew! What a day," I said as we climbed back aboard the craft. "Who would have thought! We had better get this ship back to the Complex before anything else happens."

"What was the star like?" asked Myra, once we were under way.

"Very serene and peaceful," replied Shar. "Visiting it was like a drink of pure refreshing water...but water for the soul."

"Will you take the Princess up on her invitation to visit?" I asked with a smile.

"There's a excellent chance I will," Shar said as he shifted uncomfortably in his chair. "But, before I do any more traveling I intend to get a good rest. And, I don't see any reason it can't start right now. Myra, how would you like to fly a space craft?"

"Really!!!" she squealed with delight. "You mean you will let me fly the ship?"

"Sure," he replied. "There isn't much to it. It almost flies itself. Just hold the controls gently with your hands and keep the course direction numbers on this." He pointed to a small screen directly in front of his chair. A three digit number was illuminated in red.

"I set the auto power control so there shouldn't be any deviation in speed. We have some time before we arrive at the Complex. Sealo and I will sack out on the couches, catch a short nap, and take over

The "Oh No" Trio

well before we reach the Complex. Just holler if the panel displays anything unusual."

As Myra swapped places with Shar, I made myself comfortable. As my head settled onto the soft pillow I realized how very tired I was. As I drifted off I vaguely heard Shar settle onto the adjacent couch. This is great, I thought. Little sister letting her big brothers get some much needed rest while she handles the flying...and with that thought I slipped onto the mists of a dream state.

The mists swirled caressingly around me. Every tired and tense muscle in my body began to relax and feel warm. My mind traveled toward a tinkling sound somewhere off to my left. It appeared to be voices. I moved toward it and it became louder and clearer. The mist began to lift and I saw two figures sitting on plush green grass in the middle of a flowered field beside a sparkling blue green pond. I moved closer hoping to get a clearer look. Unbelievable! One of the figures was me. The other was Ulena. We were talking and laughing. We were enjoying the warm breeze as we sat on a fluffy pale blue blanket. Spread around was an array of delicate and fragrance dishes. We were on a picnic. The sound of gentle trickling water drew my mind's eye to the stream. It was cascading over moss covered rocks from a small outcrop above us. It was making its way to join the waters of the pond. The overwhelming fragrance of flowers filled the air. My mind's eye panned the meadow and I could see that it was covered with wildflowers. The smell was exquisite.

Just then I rose from the blanket, goblet in hand, and walked to the pond. The water was sparkling and cool. I wished for a taste of its coolness to abate the heat of my blood throbbing through my chest.

Ulena sat serenely watching me. Her face was aglow with emotion. Her beauty was awe-inspiring. She had the look of one who was delighted to be with the one they love. A gentle smile came to her lips. I walked back to her side. The water had not accomplished what I had hoped. I looked down at Ulena'a angelic face and the moisture sparkling on those smiling lips. I leaned toward her thinking to taste of that moisture. I floated closer, down into her magic pool of love. Down...closer...floating. But, then I

J.L. Alonzo

began moving faster, faster, and faster. What was happening! I was falling. Something was wrong and I couldn't straighten up. I had nothing to grab onto. I had nothing to stop the fall. No! I will crash down on Ulena, spoiling the mood, the picnic...then thud!

Something was very, very wrong. I had landed on a hard flat surface, not the soft pliable body of another being. Shaking my head I opened my eyes. Everything was fuzzy but gradually focused. I was sitting on the floor of a space ship. Slowly it all came back. I must have been dreaming. Yes, I remember. We were taking the craft back to the complex. Shar and I were taking a nap. Myra was at the controls. Immediately, I jumped to my feet. Swirling my head, my eyes sought the operations area. Myra stood next the pilot's seat. She was sobbing with great tears streaming down her face. Shar was at her side, his arm around her.

"I didn't mean to," she sobbed. "You were sleeping so peacefully and soundly. I knew how tired the both of you were. I wanted to surprise you. I didn't think it would be very difficult. It was so easy flying the ship. I was sure it would be just as easy to land it. But, I couldn't get it to slow down. I couldn't get it to turn. I'm sorry! I didn't mean to hit the building! I'm so, so sorry!"

The building...she said the building. We looked out the window. There it was...the building...or at least what was left of the wall of the kitchen area. Well, we certainly made a grand return. We haven't even recovered from the last mishap and now we have something worse.

TWENTY-FIVE

So here we sit in Risan's office...the large silver desk in front of us... waiting...wondering what is in store for us this time.

Risan had been unreadable as he entered the crashed space craft. After checking to be sure we were physically all right he had simply said in a calm voice, "Meet me in my quarters."

Would we never learn? The quiet that surrounded us as we walked across the plaza had been deafening. It appeared that everyone in the Complex was present. They had been awaiting our glorious return. Yet, as I walked all I saw were shocked and solemn faces. We had completely destroyed the kitchen area, not just the outside wall. The impact was so great the wall had shattered to dust. I can only guess at what speed we had been traveling. The explosion had wiped out the interior of the cooking area. Thank goodness no one was hurt for the staff had been outside.

Myra and Shar sat stone silent on the bench beside me not even blinking. It was as if all emotion had been drained from them. I knew how they felt. I suddenly felt very old and, oh so, tired. I reached my arm out and wrapped it around Myra's shoulder. I drew her close to me and tried to comfort her. As I lowered my head to whisper my sentiments the main door to the study opened. Uncle Risan entered, followed by Uncle Shanar, Aunt Ela, my mother, and even, my grandfather, Konal. I knew we were really in for it. I tried not to show my anxiety for Myra's sake.

85

J.L. Alonzo

The adults clustered around the other side of the desk. I felt my head...and heart...sink lower and lower. I just couldn't look up. I couldn't look them in the face.

Risan's voice broke the silence. "We have made some decisions," he said. "We hope you will understand."

"Myra," he continued, "you will be put under the supervision of Ela and Sosja. They will oversee your schooling and well being. You will work with them in the Nursery until you reach the appropriate age for Fostering.

"Shar," he proceeded, "is of the age to start the Fostering program. Therefore, it has been decided that you will accompany Konal to his residence on Nistara. There you will begin your training in the areas of Intergalactic Exploration and Mediation."

"As for you, Sealo," leaning forward and placing both hands on the desk. "It has been decided that even though you are one year shy of the age requirement for Fostering, the age rule will be waived. You will be sent to your paternal grandparents on Sisteria in the Coti system. You will receive training in the areas of Education and Diplomacy."

"Much as we would have liked to have had your input in these decisions," he continued, "we felt based on some of the choices you have made recently, it was best, at this time, to handle it this way. All of these decisions were made as a group and we feel we have given your assignments careful consideration.

"Please do not misinterpret these as punishments," injected Uncle Shanar. "Fostering is a natural part of the growth for all the children of our civilization. You will go through the Ceremony of Maturing with the others. This ceremony is considered one of the most important milestones in a youth's progression to adulthood. Shar would have participated this year anyway for he is the correct age. We are sure the people will understand why you, Sealo, are doing it a little sooner than most children do. Then after the ceremony your will depart for your Fostering assignments."

Sosja stepped around the desk and took my hands in hers. Looking at me with gentle eyes, touched by sadness, she said, "You will return after you have completed your Fostering. I will visit you.

The "Oh No" Trio

But, for now, this is best. It will give the people a chance to recover from your vibrant personalities."

With a wave of Risan's hand we rose. Myra retired from the room with Ela and Sosja. Shar left with Konal and Uncle Shanar to plan for his departure. I remained frozen in place as if made of ice or stone. Would I ever learn to think things all the way through? My thoughts were flying: No more lounging in the meadow. No more feasting in the Great Hall. No more Tenacious Trio adventures. Then it really hit me, a final blow...Will I ever see Ulena again? Slowly I turned and followed Risan out the door.

My room no longer felt like the sanctuary it always had. Silently I walked around picking up my most cherished mementos. As I placed them in my luggage my mind was whirling. My thoughts were filled with sadness and regret. As I examined the small miniatures, numerous past adventures creep into my muddled brain. I have experienced some exciting things in my short life. Yet, in reality, the adventures have just begun.

Fostering is one of the most important steps in the life of an Astarian. Yes, there would be much hard work required of me, but also, there would be many new and exciting experiences that would shape my entire essence into the Being I was always meant to be.

As I glanced around my quarters double checking that everything of personal importance was packed the feeling of doom and gloom began to lift. I should be elated. With that thought I felt a slight tingle begin to trickle through my body. I would be living in the very household where my father had been born and spent his entire childhood. I would have an opportunity to build a close personal relationship with two people who, up to now, I only knew because of their title...Grandparents. This indeed would be wonderful. Fostering on Sisteria. I couldn't even begin to think of a more wish fulfilling assignment. It was only one star away from Astara and there may be opportunities for me to return from time to time.

Slowly, this new mood of happiness and excitement caused my face to tingle. As my lips turned upward in a smile, I raised my head high. I picked up my luggage and placed it beside the door. The

J.L. Alonzo

Ceremony of Maturing would be starting soon. After the reception that followed the ceremony all the participants would leave the Complex.

My lightened mind was now able to spring ahead in time. I could see myself returning to my room and collecting my luggage. I saw me walking briskly out of the room, down the hall, and out the Great Doors. I could see the awaiting space ship and, beyond that a wonderfully exciting future.

THE END

LaVergne, TN USA
08 November 2010
204029LV00002B/1/P